Another 48 HRS.™

A Novel by DEBORAH CHIEL
Story by FRED BRAUGHTON
Screenplay by JOHN FASANO & JEB STUART
and LARRY GROSS

POCKET BOOKS
New York London Toronto Sydney Tokyo Singapore

This book is a work of fiction. Names, characters, places and incidents are either the product of the author's imagination or are used fictitiously. Any resemblance to actual events or locales or persons, living or dead, is entirely coincidental.

An *Original* publication of POCKET BOOKS

POCKET BOOKS, a division of Simon & Schuster Inc.
1230 Avenue of the Americas, New York, NY 10020

ISBN: 0-671-72573-4

First Pocket Books printing July 1990

10 9 8 7 6 5 4 3 2 1

Printed in the U.S.A.

REGGIE WAS SMILING AS HE WALKED TOWARD THE MAIN PRISON GATE—AND FREEDOM.

His face went flat when he saw Jack Cates waiting for him.

"Get out of here." Reggie dismissed him and kept right on walking. "We got nothin' to talk about until I get my money."

"Told you yesterday. You're not gettin' it unless you help me," Cates calmly replied. "I been chasing a drug dealer called the Iceman for four years. Last week I found out he wants you dead. That makes you the best lead I've ever had."

Reggie stared at Cates as if the cop had lost his marbles. "Helping you out, when you're keepin' my money *and* my Porsche, is the last thing I want to do," he spat.

"Look," Cates yelled back, "I got forty-eight hours to bring in this guy, or I'm history."

That got Reggie's attention. "You want me to go with you for *another* forty-eight hours? No way!"

Cates grabbed Reggie's arm. "I promise you, this time, it's gonna be different. I don't just lose my badge . . . I go to jail."

"You in trouble with the law?" Reggie hooted. "Good. *Good!* Bad as I feel about you keepin' my money, that almost makes up for it." Reggie turned to take one last look at the stone walls of the prison. "Don't worry, Jack. I'll come back here in five or six years and visit you. . . ."

• 1

One day passes pretty much the same as the next for a con doing time. The smart ones numb themselves to the harsh discipline and monotony of prison life. They learn to ignore the insults and petty humiliations served up by guards who get their kicks by busting ass. They draw big black *X*'s on the calendar, keeping track of the weeks and months still to go until that magic moment when their name is called, the gates swing open, and they're free to go. They watch their backs, try to keep their noses clean, and make sure they don't get caught when there's trouble.

It's a boring, soul-deadening, blues-singing existence, especially for the cons serving hard time in a prison on the road to nowhere. Nothing but grassy, rolling fields stretch out for miles in all directions. The wind blows hot by day, cold by night. The only other signs of life are an occasional hawk gliding by overhead in search of prey, or a herd of wild horses that's strayed too near the prison walls.

And then one morning a man screams loudly enough to be heard halfway across the exercise yard. A siren wails. The cellblock doors slam shut. The guards curse and yell and hit the ground running. Eventually order is restored, and punishments are meted out. Life returns to normal—whatever "normal" may be for the cons living out their days behind barbed-wire-crested walls.

On one such morning, an inmate at Folsom State Prison dropped to the floor, doubled over with pain, and began to scream as if he were teetering on the brink of hell. The two medical orderlies were tough guys who thought they'd seen it all. But even they couldn't help but be impressed by the amount of blood gushing from between the wounded con's thighs as they hoisted him onto a hospital gurney.

Moments earlier they'd thrown a sheet across his bare midsection, and already it was stained bright red and was soaking wet. Somebody had put a knife to the guy's groin and carved it up like a Thanksgiving turkey.

The younger orderly, new and less hardened by the job, shook his head in amazement. "What the hell is this?" he asked his more experienced buddy as they steered the gurney through the dingy corridor toward the double doors of the infirmary.

"Attempted rape!" the older con shouted above the wounded man's shrieks.

"Jesus Christ!" swore his pal. He would have hated to see what a successful rape would have looked like. "They get the rapist?"

The kid had a lot to learn, thought the older con. He chuckled to himself as he answered the question. "This *is* the rapist."

Elsewhere in the same prison, in a small, windowless detention room, another con sat alone at a table. The unpainted stone walls of the room were dank and mildewed. The high-intensity bulb that hung low from the ceiling was positioned to provide the maximum discomfort for the person being interrogated.

The handsome young black man seated at the table seemed not to notice either the rank, moldy odor that permeated the room, or the unpleasantly bright light. Certainly he paid no attention to the face peering in at him through the barred window of the door. With eyes half-shut as if he were catnapping, he leaned back in the chair, folded his arms across his chest, and tapped his foot softly in time to the song that ran through his head.

Only when the door burst open did he glance up. With a slight nod of his head, he coolly acknowledged the presence of the prison warden, a grim-faced man with thinning hair, bushy eyebrows, and a mouth that was set in a permanently disapproving straight line.

The warden had been up late partying at his favorite bar. Drinking too many whiskeys on an empty stomach had left him with a nasty hangover this morning. He'd planned to take it easy—until this jerkoff had gone knife-happy and screwed up his day. With the taste of stale booze still on his tongue, he found a spot for himself just outside the circle of light and stared reprovingly at the con, as a teacher might stare at a small child who had gravely disappointed him. Then he opened up a manila file folder and began to read aloud from it.

"February, 1985. Two thousand seven hundred dollars stolen from San Quentin Prison accounting office." He glanced at the con to make sure he was listening. "They found the money in your cell, your sentence was extended five years, and you were transferred here."

Reggie Hammond barely stifled a yawn of boredom. *Tell me something I* don't *know,* he thought.

"I know," the warden said impatiently. "You were set up. Always the same thing from you—it's never your fault. Well, *this* time it is your fault. One week to go on your sentence and you decide to mutilate another inmate. That's very stupid. Why'd you do it?"

Reggie leaned forward on his elbows and rested his chin on top of his folded hands. "Aw, c'mon, man!" he loudly objected. "I didn't have no choice, that's why."

His warm brown eyes radiating sincerity, he creased his lips into the smile that had seduced a thousand ladies and looked up at the warden. In his standard-issue blue uniform, he could have been posing for a picture as model prisoner of the month.

The warden didn't much like Reggie Hammond, who had a mouth on him the size of Texas and a swelled head to match. Still, he did have a grudging respect for Hammond's intelligence. And compared to most of the jerks and sickos who'd found their way into his prison, Hammond was a goddamned Boy Scout. Except this time he'd forgotten his manners, and the warden wasn't buying any of his bullshit.

Reggie could see that the warden needed to have it spelled out for him. Smoothing his moustache, he went on. "Where I come from, if you're in a cell with someone, and they start running toward you with their dick in one hand and a knife in the other, that means you got a problem, and I didn't want to get stuck by either one. No way!"

Pausing for breath, he glared at the warden.

"Nobody's turning me out—and nobody's checking me out. I walked into this bullshit institution you run on my own two feet. I plan on goin' out the same way. . . . You got me?"

High on the long list of things Reggie hated about being a con were the overgrown apes, otherwise known as guards, whose balls were attached to their guns. Like the two assholes who were dragging him down the hall like a goddamned sack of Idaho potatoes when he was perfectly willing to walk on his own two feet. They were treating him as if he was some kind of troublemaker, instead of seeing him for the potential victim that he was.

"You screwed up big this time, Hammond," the warden told him as he kept pace alongside his prisoner. "Attempted murder's bigger than robbery."

"Self-defense!" Reggie protested, struggling to free his arms.

The warden snorted. "Nobody's going to buy that."

Reggie felt a dangerous volcano of rage boiling up inside him. He shrugged himself free of the guards, stared the warden straight in the eye.

"I served two years for a crime I did. I never denied that shit," he said hotly. "But I already spent five years I never should have. I never robbed that payroll, and I cut that dude to save my life. You got murderers in here who served less time than me. Unless you're a complete fucker, you'll let me out in a week, like you're supposed to."

The warden's head felt as if somebody had clamped a vise around it. He wanted nothing more than to get back to his office, swallow some aspirin, and send out for a cold six-pack. Hammond and his bullshit stories had already taken up too much of his day.

On the other hand, once you got past Hammond's big fat mouth, he wasn't a troublemaker. He usually did what he was supposed to, minded his own business, kept his hands clean. The bloodbath that morning was totally out of character. Maybe some asshole on the outside did want him dead.

What if that were true, and today's little escapade earned him a few more years in the slammer? A ten-thousand-dollar contract added up to a lot of spare change. Hammond would be a sitting duck for every crazy hired gun who walked through the prison doors.

And who'd get stuck cleaning up the mess? Who'd have to answer to the hotshots up in Sacramento if a con left the joint in a body bag before he was finished paying his debt to society? He would, because he was the goddamned warden. Hell, he had more important things to do than testify before a state commission on prison reform.

So what if Hammond had whacked off a piece of another con's dick? The guy probably had plenty to spare.

The warden reached a well-considered decision. "I think," he said, almost tasting the beer in his mouth, "that it would be best if you spent your remaining time here in isolation."

Reggie hid his triumphant grin as the guards grabbed his arms and dragged him away. His granny, who'd raised him almost from the day he was born, had always said he knew how to speechify. All those times he'd talked his way out of going to yet another prayer meeting. Poor Granny. What if she were alive to see him now? She'd had her heart set on his becoming a preacher. But Reggie somehow had known from a very early age that his talents lay elsewhere. He was still waiting to exploit them fully.

The door of the isolation cell slammed shut with a loud *clunk!* that reverberated along the length of the otherwise empty corridor. Normally, that was one of the loneliest sounds a con could ever hear—but today it was music to Reggie's ears. Like Garbo, he "vanted to be alone," at least for one more week, until his time was up. Alone, he was safe. Alone, he didn't have to be watching his back for stray knives or bullets.

A week in isolation was an extremely small price to pay for getting out alive. And Reggie had a lot to live for.

He took a look around, examining his new, temporary quarters. The cell was cramped and dark. It was lit only by a dim bulb and a muted shaft of light that shone through the narrow observation hole toward the top of the door. The furnishings consisted of a toilet, a sink, and a sagging mattress covered by a thin blanket. In the corner near the toilet, several generations of cockroaches were doing their thing.

Reggie had seen worse, though not much. But what the fuck? Seven days in the black hole of Calcutta, and then Reggie Hammond would be O-U-T out of there. And he'd finally have himself some serious good times. First, he'd liberate his money and his car from Jack Cates. Maybe he'd hang around long enough to punch out that fucker a time or two. Next, he'd find himself some pussy—and he'd keep on screwing for as long as it took to make up for the last five years.

So he'd been dealt a bum deal. Another man might have stored up his anger and plotted revenge. But rage had a way of gnawing at one's soul, leaving one with nothing to show the world but a small, hard kernel of bitterness. That wasn't Reggie's style. He was cool.

Stretching out on the mattress, he closed his eyes and contemplated the lady of his dreams: beautiful, sexy, a good dancer with an easy smile and a great pair of tits. She'd be waiting for him at the bar in one of his favorite clubs, wishing that a guy like him would walk through the door. He'd buy her a drink and quickly work his magic with her, as he had with countless other girls.

They always giggled when they cuddled up to him in bed. "Honey, where'd you get your smile and that cute little butt? Do it to me again, baby," they'd beg, reaching for him under the covers. And, of course, he'd oblige, because one thing a man could never get too much of was pussy.

Or money. Soon he'd have plenty of that. He knew exactly how he was going to spend it. Clothes. Food. Wine. A pad he could be proud of. Reggie had expensive tastes, and he couldn't wait to indulge himself. Whatever was left over, he'd invest. Then he'd sit back and watch his fortune grow.

Ah, yes, indeed. Reggie had a *whole* lot to live for.

Sighing with impatience, he kicked off his shoes and folded his hands behind his head. In an off-key, screechy falsetto, he began to wail the song that had gotten him through so many other long, sleepless, horny nights. His theme song, one might say.

"Roxanne, you don't have to put on the red light . . . Roxanne, walk the streets for money . . . you don't even care if it's wrong or if it's right . . ."

• 2

A merciless midday sun beat down on the barren desert landscape. Waves of heat shimmered in the distance. The air was close and utterly still, except for an occasional gust of wind that threw up gritty clouds of thick, brown dust. A narrow dirt road, hardly the width of one car, stretched toward the horizon, cutting a crooked swath through the shifting dunes. A person could drive through the desert for eight, ten hours at a stretch and never see another human being.

The only sign of life for miles around was a weather-beaten cantina that functioned as a combination gas station, greasy spoon, bar, and pool hall. This one-stop oasis was a sad, low-slung building fronted by a ramshackle porch, an old-fashioned hitching post, and a wind wheel that listed precariously as it strained to catch the breeze. Except for the odd tourist passing through on his way back to civilization, the customers were mostly local cowboys and outlaws who cared only that the drinks were strong and the food was cheap.

They were hard-looking, silent men whose pasts were better forgotten. Few secrets got spilled across the scarred redwood bar. The bartender, a thin, stoop-shouldered man with deep-set eyes, had secrets of his own that had brought him to the desert. He wasn't easily frightened. But he had a good nose for smelling trouble—and the stranger at the table by the window was giving off a strong scent of danger.

He was a big fellow who'd pulled up on a late-model Harley, and he had the kind of hard, impassive expression that deliberately discouraged even the most casual conversation. As his fingers returned again and again to stroke his carefully groomed Fu Manchu moustache, he couldn't seem to tear his gaze away from the view beyond the dirt-streaked windows. From that, and the way he'd surveyed the otherwise empty cantina when he'd walked in a few minutes earlier, the bartender guessed that the stranger was expecting company.

"Hey, mister," he said, "you want to have a beer or somethin' while you're waitin'?"

There was no response. He might as well have been talking to himself.

"Hey," he repeated, "can you hear me, mister?"

The stranger, who called himself Malcolm Price, had just found what he'd been looking for out in the desert. He turned away from the window and grunted an assent. "Tequila. The bottle."

"Sure. Sure thing." The bartender smiled obligingly and poured a generous shot for the stranger. "Maybe

I'll join you," he said, filling a second glass. A good drink, tequila. Good for passing a long, dull afternoon.

Up the road by a battered mailbox, a young biker, Willie Hickok, leaned against his black Harley, waiting for his friend. Willie had greasy, shoulder-length hair, a skull-and-crossbones earring in his left ear, a stubbly two-day-old beard, and blue eyes that squinted behind dark sunglasses as he watched a second Harley come into focus through the heat ripples. The bike tore down the dirt road, churning up angry cyclones of sand until it roared to a stop next to the mailbox.

Hickok picked up his saddlebag and waved a greeting at his pal. Cherry Ganz was about the same age as Hickok, in his mid-twenties, and was similarly dressed in dirty, faded jeans, a sweat-stained T-shirt, a neck bandanna to catch the dust, and a well-worn leather jacket. He was a tall man, with a wiry, muscular build and the gaunt-faced look of a man who had learned to expect the worst out of life. He sported a beard and a moustache, and a tattoo marked his left cheek, just below his eye—a single teardrop.

Now he jumped off his bike in a hurry and slapped hands with Hickok. Without exchanging a word, the two men headed toward the cantina. Whatever news they had to share could wait until they'd talked to Price.

The bartender had seen them coming and figured they'd be thirsty. "Howdy, fellas. What can I do for you?" he asked.

"Brewskis," said Hickok. He'd been riding into the sun since dawn, and now it took a few moments for his eyes to adjust to the dimly lit bar. Swigging down the icy beer, he searched the shadows until he found Price.

He nodded at Ganz to join him. "I always hate a fella that's not on time," Hickok drawled, pulling up a chair.

Price offered Hickok his hand. "Been a while, Willie." He nodded at Ganz.

"Monterey. Gas was cheap, asses were kicked." Hickok smiled briefly at the memory.

But neither man had traveled this far into the desert to catch up on old times. They were business associates, not friends, and their mutual cordiality was mostly for show. Hickok wanted to see the color of Price's money, and Price knew it.

He reached for the saddlebag that he'd brought with him into the cantina and threw back the flap to reveal a sea of hundred-dollar bills, held together by elastic bands. "Fifty now. Fifty more when you're done," he said.

Ganz moved closer, like a hawk moving in for the kill. He stared hungrily at the bills. "How many?" he demanded.

"Just one," Price said.

A hundred thousand was a shitload of dough for getting rid of just one guy. "What is he . . . another cop?" asked Ganz.

Price had been looking forward to springing this little surprise on Ganz. "Nope, not a cop. Matter of fact," he told him, "he's a friend of yours. You're gonna like this job."

He unfolded a piece of paper. It was a police I.D. picture, complete with the suspect's number below his unsmiling mug shot. The photograph was creased and smudged, as if someone had carried it around for a long time. But Ganz immediately recognized the face.

"Shit!" he said softly.

Hickok threw him a questioning glance. Did he know the guy?

"He was in the same gang as my brother," Ganz explained. "First he dropped a dime on him. After that he ratted on him to the cop that blew him away."

Oh, yeah, he knew that motherfucker. And Price was so dumb he didn't realize Ganz would have killed him for nothing.

"He's still got all his nigger friends protectin' him inside. But once he gets out, he's yours," said Price, congratulating himself on having suggested Ganz for the job.

Hickok liked the sound of this setup. Another couple of beers, and he'd be ready to shake on the deal. He looked up to signal the bartender and got distracted by a car pulling up in front of the cantina.

"Hey!" He jerked his head toward the window. Ganz followed his gaze and swore angrily. Price quickly covered up the money and shoved the saddlebag under the table.

Just what they didn't need. The goddamned California Highway Patrol.

If it hadn't been for the black Harleys gleaming in the sunlight, the cops probably would have driven right by the cantina. They were coming into the home stretch of an uneventful shift, and they'd already written up their quota of tickets for the month. But the bikes beckoned to them like a couple of whores working the street on a Saturday night.

"They look kind of nasty," said the cop in the passenger's seat. A gutsy lady with a deceptively sweet face, she'd run into enough bikers to know that more than one Harley in any given locale usually added up to trouble.

The cop in the driver's seat nodded. "We better run the plates," he said, pulling off the road.

"I'll take a look and be right back," volunteered the lady cop, who was still out to prove that she was as tough as any man on the force. "Want a soda?"

"Yeah, diet," said the driver.

He picked up the radio mike and flicked the On switch. "This is seventeen Adam ninety-one," he identified himself as his partner disappeared inside the cantina.

There was a burst of static, then the disembodied voice of the dispatcher. "Go ahead, A-ninety-one."

"We're on the Simmons trail about fifteen miles west off Route Fourteen. I need Wants and Warrants on two motorcycle registrations. First one is California, six, David, eight, four, Sam, niner."

"Copy, six, David, eight, four, Sam, niner," echoed the dispatcher.

"Second plate. California, niner, Robert, two, seven, Baker, one."

"Copy," the dispatcher replied. "Niner, Robert, two, seven, Baker, one. Hold on for D.M.V./N.C.I.C. check."

"Right," said the cop. He leaned back against his seat, kept one eye on the cantina door, and waited for the computer to spit out whatever it might have on the guys who owned those babies.

The lady cop could sense the tension in the air as soon as she walked into the cantina. She glanced around, then nodded at the bartender. "Tom."

The bartender smiled weakly. "Nice seein' you," he told her.

The lady cop's eyes settled on the three men seated by the window. Her sister in Bakersfield had been beaten up by a biker a couple of years back. Since then, the cop had welcomed any opportunity to hassle those tattooed sons-of-bitches. Here was as unappealing a trio as she'd ever come across. They didn't much look as if they were wanting any company. With any luck, she'd have the pleasure of busting up the party and ruining their fun.

Hickok watched her saunter across the room and wondered what she looked like beneath her uniform. He stood as she approached them. "Yes, ma'am. Willie Hickok. I'm right here," he said with an insolent grin.

"Officer," Ganz volunteered, getting to his feet. He wanted to play, too. "Cherry Ganz."

The lady cop carefully studied his face, then, just as carefully, eyeballed the other two. Finally, she said, "Do I know you guys?"

Ganz whipped out his shiny chrome .44 Magnum and fired the gun twice at point-blank range. The lady cop barely had time to cry out before the bullets slammed into her chest. The explosion hurtled her body backward against the window, shattering the glass on impact.

"Later," said Ganz, saluting her with his trigger finger. He sprinted after Hickok, who was already rushing through the cantina door to take care of her partner.

The other cop was there to greet them with his shotgun raised and ready. But Hickok was quicker. His handgun blazing, he stormed outside and blasted the cop with a spray of bullets that sent him flying across the top of his car. He landed with his legs dangling over the windshield and a stream of blood gushing out of his mouth.

"He's dead," said Hickok.

Just to be sure, Ganz took aim between the cop's eyes and fired one last shot. The man's face was instantly transformed from one with human features into a macabre jigsaw puzzle of blood-soaked cartilage and scorched flesh.

After all the gunfire, there was a moment of sudden stillness. Then the car radio came alive. "California, six, David, eight, four, Sam, niner. Registered to Hickok, William. Expired eight eighty-seven. Wanted: two counts armed robbery, Los Angeles County. Armed robbery, Orange County. Car theft, Mesa County. No present address. Presumed armed." The dispatcher took a breath, then droned on. "California, niner, Robert, two, seven, Baker, one. Registered to Ganz, Richard, aka 'Cherry.' Registration expired ten eighty-eight. Wanted: three counts armed robbery, Orange County. Five counts assault, Ventura County. Car theft, Mesa County. Seventy-two open traffic summonses. No present address. Presumed armed and dangerous."

Ganz had heard enough. If he wanted to publicize his credentials, he could take out an ad in a newspaper. He raised his gun and fired at the radio. Whatever else the dispatcher had to say was lost forever in the explosion.

Price had watched the shootout from inside the cantina. He'd never seen Ganz and Hickok in action. They were crazy sons-of-bitches, that was for damn sure. But they knew how to handle their guns, and they were quick on their feet. Maybe they really could pull off the job he'd just hired them to do.

There had been another witness to the gunplay—Tom the bartender, who was more interested in saving his hide than in admiring the bikers' marksmanship. As soon as the bullets began to fly, he dived for shelter behind the bar and prayed that none of the bullets would ricochet in his direction.

In all the excitement, Price had almost forgotten about him. Now, however, his attention was caught by the familiar clicking sound of a telephone being dialed. He tracked the noise to its source and peered over the top of the bar.

"Who ya callin', friend?" he asked the bartender, who was crouched on the floor.

The bartender glanced up and swallowed hard at the sight of Price's gleaming .44 Magnum. "Nobody! Nobody!" he insisted, his voice quavering.

Price leveled the gun and demanded, "You wouldn't call the cops on us here, would ya?"

"No! No!" shrieked the terrified man. "I won't tell! I hate cops! I won't tell."

"I don't believe you," Price said, taunting the bartender. He cocked the gun and released the safety with a loud click.

"No!! Noooo . . . !"

The bartender's screams ended abruptly in a hollow death rattle as a single bullet exploded in his throat and severed his windpipe.

Price grabbed his saddlebagful of money, put away his gun, and strolled outside to join his friends.

• 3

It was six A.M. on a typical day at the Hunter's Point racetrack, southeast of San Francisco. The sun had barely risen, and the sky was still more gray than blue. But the air was already thick with the smell of gas and the roar of overrevved engines. Souped-up motorcycles circled the half-mile oval of oil-streaked dirt. Daredevil drivers, wearing leather jackets and heavily padded boots, leaned low to the ground, negotiating the unbanked turn at dizzying speeds. A few diehard fans, mostly bikers, had scattered themselves across the grandstand and were breakfasting on beer and cigarettes.

The track mechanics had arrived early as usual. Leaning up against the tall bales of hay that ringed the track, they'd drunk their coffee and had their morning gossip. Now they were at their stations in the infield pits, checking the oil, changing tires, tightening bolts. The mechanics, most of them young men with tough faces and even tougher hands, were the unsung heroes of the track; their sharp-eyed maintenance of the bikes often meant the difference between a safe race and a disaster.

One mechanic, however, stood idle and alone by a gas pump, uninvolved in the bustle of activity taking place on and off the track. A slightly built man with a sharp nose and a face like a weasel, he couldn't seem to tear his eyes away from the infield gate, except to glance occasionally at the scruffy gym bag resting at his feet. The bikes zoomed past him more times than he could count before he spotted a thin, black man dressed in a brown raincoat, strolling through the gate. He gave a brief nod of recognition. This had to be his guy.

He'd said his name was Burroughs when they'd talked on the phone. No first name, but he didn't need one. What mattered was that he worked for the Iceman. He said he'd be wearing a light brown raincoat and carrying a briefcase. "You'll know me," Burroughs had said with an unpleasant laugh. "I'm sure you don't bump into too many black men out there at the Point."

Burroughs was a cool customer with suspicious eyes glinting out from behind his glasses, a sloping forehead, and a thin, tight mouth that had almost forgotten how to smile. He'd outlived a lot of bad characters, and the secret of his survival was that he trusted no one, least of all the Iceman. But he did the man's bidding and was well paid for his services.

He also had a nose for trouble that had served him well through many long days and nights on the street.

Now he glanced around, his senses finely attuned to danger. A couple of pit mechanics were doing a quick wheel change on a Harley a few feet from where he stood. Burroughs glared in their direction.

But the man Burroughs had come to meet shook his head to indicate he shouldn't worry. They were so engrossed in their job that they didn't even bother to look up when their co-worker and Burroughs walked past them, looking for a quiet place to talk.

By unspoken agreement, the two men stopped next to a pyramid of fifty-five-gallon oil drums that fed the gas pumps positioned at intervals around the perimeter of the track. Burroughs rested his briefcase on top of the gas pump. He flipped it open and gestured to the mechanic to inspect the contents. Then he reiterated the terms of the deal. "Hundred thousand for the job. Fifty thousand now. Iceman's a generous guy."

The mechanic was used to doing complicated repairs that required a steady hand. But now his fingers trembled as he dug into the briefcase and withdrew a bundle of green bills. He rubbed his hand against his grease-stained blue overalls, calculating his value to the Iceman.

"Don't like hundreds," he said sullenly. "I told you that before. What kind of shit is this?"

The mechanic threw the bills back into the briefcase and glared at the Iceman's messenger.

His show of bravado was wasted on Burroughs. The guy had gambling debts up the wazoo and a checking account that was registering near empty. This dude was headed for extinction unless he suddenly came into some major money. Burroughs inspected his carefully buffed fingernails.

"Oh, yeah? That right?" He faked a yawn. "Go ahead. Make your play."

His bluff called, the mechanic reconsidered quickly and decided that he could live with whatever Burroughs had brought him. "Just kidding," he said. He quickly began transferring the money from the briefcase into his gym bag.

"This is the guy," said Burroughs, sticking a police I.D. photograph under the mechanic's nose. "The balance when he's dusted, you know what I mean? Too bad for this cat, we want him dead."

The mechanic grabbed the photo and stuck it inside the gym bag. "Yeah, whatever. No problem," he promised.

He could study the picture later. Right now he was more concerned with stashing the money and getting back to work before anyone started asking questions. Burroughs was right about one thing. With his fancy raincoat and black skin, he wasn't exactly inconspicuous. If he didn't hurry up and disappear, they'd soon be attracting a whole lot of attention that wouldn't do either of them any good.

The bad news was that they already had an audience who'd arrived at the track at about the time the mechanic was crawling out of bed. The witness was a big bear of a man. He had a nose that looked as if it had taken a punch or two, a bull neck, and broad shoulders that strained the back of his jacket. But he moved with surprising grace as he stalked the two men from behind the stacks of baled hay.

It had been a long, chilly wait. But now that the money had changed hands, the man had seen enough. He had his two suspects right where he wanted them.

Grasping his nickel-plated .44 Magnum in two oversized fists, he thrust his muscular arms in front of him as he emerged from behind the haystacks.

"Freeze!" yelled the man, whose name was Jack Cates. "Police officer!"

Burroughs and the mechanic turned and gaped at him, panic in their eyes.

"You! Move a step apart!" Cates ordered, motioning to them with his gun. "Slow! I don't want anybody to get hurt—"

The two men suddenly sprang into action. Briefcase in hand, Burroughs took off at a sprint. The mechanic pulled out a small revolver and took quick, careful aim. Cates dropped to the greasy pavement only seconds before the bullet flew through the air above his head. The mechanic never had a chance to go for round two. Cates raised his gun. The Magnum blasted once . . . twice . . . three times.

The first two shots slammed the mechanic square in the chest with such force that he was pushed off his feet and tossed backward like a floppy rag doll. He hit the ground screaming with pain and with blood spraying from him. He was still screaming when the third shot slammed into the gas pump.

A loud, ominous *whoosh* rumbled up from the depths of the pump.

Jack Cates hadn't heard that particular noise for twenty-odd years, not since the days when he'd been a roustabout on an oil rig off the coast of Louisiana. It was a sound no sane man ever wanted to hear twice in his life; Cates, for all his idiosyncrasies, still fell under the clinical definition of *compos mentis.*

He hit the dirt just as the gas pump erupted with a

deafening clap, sending shock waves through the ground. Angry orange flames exploded in every direction. A massive fireball snaked along the floor in the direction of the wounded mechanic, as resolutely as the needle of a compass seeking true North. He pitched sideways, trying to roll out of its path. But the ten-foot-high flame, like a dragon needing to be fed, swallowed him into its searing, hot depths. He stumbled to his feet, a human torch shrieking for help.

Armed with fire extinguishers, the well-trained pit mechanics had already come running to put out the blaze. Jack jumped to his feet and scrambled to catch up with Burroughs. Acrid billows of black smoke clogged his nose and mouth. His eyes were tearing and he was gasping for air by the time he cleared the pit area.

Burroughs had gotten a good head start. He was running fast and hard, and he had the advantage on Cates, a two-pack-a-day cigarette smoker who wasn't built for speed. When Cates spotted him, he was halfway across the track, headed for the infield gate.

A crowd of bikes whizzed by at breakneck speed, stirring up thick swirls of dust. Onlookers shouted angry warnings at Cates as he leaped onto the track. But he was oblivious to the danger. He took aim and screamed, "Freeze or you're—"

The rest of his threat was drowned out by a thunderous roar of engines. A second pack of bikes tore around the curve, heading for Cates. He tumbled out of their path just as the lead driver swerved to avoid him.

There was a screech of brakes and the smell of burning rubber. The next bike in line plowed into the leader and slid sideways across the track, letting a spray of sparks fly. The guy behind him tried to play Evel Kneivel and landed head first in the mud.

When the dust settled, four monster bikes lay on their sides in the dirt, a tangled mess of steel and rubber. Burroughs was long gone.

Jack picked himself up off the ground and let out a world-class stream of curses. One arm was bruised from the fall he'd taken, and his jacket was covered with grease and bits of straw. But he was too angry to notice the damage. He'd come *that* close to catching the bastards. Now one of them had slipped through his fingers, and the other was probably dead . . .

Or maybe not. Cursing every step of the way, Cates stomped back toward the gas pump where track workers were battling the still-fiery blaze with chemical extinguishers.

"Get back!" they shouted at him. "Get the hell out of here!"

Cates flipped them the finger and glanced at the man he'd shot. The mechanic lay on the ground covered in a piece of shiny, silver material that was meant to keep him from going into shock. Several of the other mechanics were crouched around him, waiting for the ambulance to arrive. From the looks of it, he wouldn't be doing much talking for a while—if ever.

Police sirens screeched shrilly in the distance. In another minute or two, the cops would be all over the place, asking questions. If there were clues to be found, Cates wanted to get his hands on them before his pals showed up.

He picked his way through the ashes and debris,

dodging the flames that licked at his scuffed cowboy boots.

"What the hell are you doing?" yelled one of the pit men.

Cates ignored him. He bent down and poked around inside the mechanic's scorched gym bag, which had managed to survive the explosion more or less intact.

Bingo! His fingers closed around the torn piece of paper Burroughs had given the mechanic. It was a photograph, badly singed around the edges. Cates could just barely make out the face.

He had to look again, hardly believing what he saw. It was none other than his old friend, Reggie Hammond.

The ambulances got there first, though they were too late for the mechanic. Next the squad cars started pouring through the gates. The guys from Homicide arrived soon afterward. The fire was finally out, the pump reduced to a twisted, blackened husk that could have passed for a modern-art sculpture. Jack sat back and watched his fellow cops crawl all over the place like ants on spilled sugar.

He grimaced when he saw Inspector Blake Wilson step out of his unmarked brown sedan. Naturally Wilson had made a beeline for the track as soon as the story had come over the police radio. It wasn't as if he gave a shit about a couple of smashed bikes or one less pit mechanic in the world. His presence on the scene had everything to do with Jack Cates.

A vain man who put on airs about knowing the best restaurants and the right wines to drink, Wilson was a bit of a joke among the other cops. As head of the watchdog Internal Affairs Department, however, he wielded a lot of power. Few of his colleagues were either brave or foolish enough to laugh in his face. Jack was proud to count himself among that minority.

This morning Wilson was smoothly shaved and clad in a dapper way as usual in a dark suit and a perfectly pressed white shirt. His silk tie was held firmly in place by a gold-and-diamond tie clasp that glinted in the sunlight. His sharp demeanor was in marked contrast with that of Officer Joe Stevens, the sloppily dressed, potbellied plainclothesman who was questioning one of the bikers.

"So explain to me exactly what happened," Stevens was saying, nodding a hello to Wilson.

"It's like this," answered the biker, tugging off his leather gloves. "And comin' around the turn, and all of a sudden this big guy is standing in the middle o' the track waving his gun around like he was crazy. Next thing I know I'm eatin' some guy's tailpipe. . . ."

"Wait a minute. Slow down," Stevens said, scribbling notes. "Tell it to me slow."

The biker shrugged and started over again. "He's in the middle of the track, waving a gun—"

"Stevens!" Wilson broke in, stepping between the biker and the cop. "What the hell happened here?"

"It's kind of messy, sir," Stevens replied.

"Details! You want to give me some details?"

"Jack Cates took down one of the locals," Stevens said reluctantly. "A slug hit the gas pump . . . and burned the bad guy to a crisp. Jack claims it was a righteous shoot."

"So what's the problem?" demanded Wilson.

Stevens looked uncomfortable. Why did he have to be the one to get quizzed by I.A.D.? Finally he admitted, "So far they can't find the french fry's gun."

Wilson nodded at Stevens to keep up the good work and moved on.

The biker, meanwhile, was getting impatient. "Let me ask you, who's going to take care of my bike?" he wanted to know.

Stevens slammed his notebook shut. He'd had about as much as he could take of this character. "You got insurance, don't you?" he snarled.

Ben Kehoe, who considered himself a friend of Jack's, had been supervising the search for evidence in the immediate vicinity of the fire. One very important piece was missing. Unless it turned up, Wilson would have the perfect excuse to jump all over Cates.

Kehoe was a hawk-nosed, foul-mouthed cop, given to wearing loud ties and playing practical jokes. But he looked perfectly serious now as he walked over to where Cates had perched himself on top of an oil drum. Kehoe broke the bad news. "So far we can't find the gun, Jack."

Cates shrugged unconcernedly. He was certain of two things. One, the mechanic had taken a shot at him. Two, bullets didn't come flying out of a man's finger. You didn't, therefore, need a detective's badge to figure out that the man had a gun. In the confusion that followed the explosion, the gun had disappeared. But it existed, and Cates had no reason to doubt that it would soon come to light.

Two paramedics walked by. They were carrying a body bag that contained what was left of the mechanic.

"Christ! You really toasted this guy," said Kehoe, a hint of admiration in his voice.

Cates and Kehoe went back a long way. They'd been rookies together on the force, moved up through the ranks, and earned their promotions at more or less the same time. Their desks were within shouting distance of each other.

If asked, Cates would have described Kehoe as a damned fine cop, a man to be trusted in an emergency. Depending on who wanted to know, he might have also added that the man had a twisted sense of humor and an outstanding talent for sticking his foot in his mouth. These particular traits had never set well with Cates, who held to the belief that the less said the better.

Kehoe's crack about the mechanic was a good case in point. Most likely he hadn't been anyone's definition of a great human being, but Cates didn't get off on killing people. When he did so, it was only because he was a cop, doing his job. Kehoe was a jerk, everyone knew that. Still, his comment bugged Cates.

"Goddammit! I didn't toast the guy. I just shot him," he protested. "Chrissakes, he toasted himself, Ben."

"Calm down, Jack. We'll find the gun. We just gotta do this. Get our stories straight." Kehoe smiled reassuringly and patted Cates on the arm.

Stories? thought Jack. *There are no* stories. *There's a goddamned gun, is what there is.*

"All right," he said grudgingly, pulling out his cigarettes. "I was on a stakeout—"

"Hey, Jack." Frank Cruise, another of the detectives in his squad, interrupted him. "I checked the guy's locker. Nothing unusual in his I.D. He checks out. Works here at the track, fifty bucks in his wallet, pair of sunglasses. Some keys—car and apartment. Still haven't found his gun, though."

"Shit!" muttered Kehoe, catching sight of Wilson a few yards away. "It's that bastard Wilson. Let me talk to him, Jack."

"No. No, it's my deal. I'll take care of it," Cates said flatly. He didn't need anyone to fight his battles, least of all Kehoe.

"Man, I hate these I.A.D. scumbags," Cruise grumbled. The worry lines across his forehead deepened, and he played nervously with his pinky ring. Cruise's father, who'd also been a policeman, had instilled in him a deep suspicion of cops who ratted on their colleagues. As far as Cruise was concerned, the Internal Affairs Department was the final resting place for cops who didn't have the brains to be detectives.

So there were no warm welcomes, no slaps on the back, when Wilson joined the three detectives. Wilson couldn't have cared less. He hadn't signed on with the I.A.D. in order to win popularity contests.

Although he didn't need any introduction, he flipped open his I.D. and said, "Blake Wilson, Internal Affairs Division. Hello, Jack. Seems like I'm always running into you."

"Yeah," Cates mumbled, ignoring Wilson's outstretched hand. "I can't take a leak without one of your boys watching me."

"Give us a minute, fellas," Wilson said, glancing pointedly at Cruise and Kehoe, who quickly backed away. Wilson fished in his pocket for his cigarettes and made a big deal out of lighting up. Finally, with just a hint of exasperation in his tone, he said, "So what did you do now, Jack?"

"I was on a stakeout. I was getting real close—"

"Oh, no. Not the Iceman!"

"Yeah, goddammit. The Iceman. I'm getting close," Jack insisted. "I'm gonna nail this guy."

"For four years you've been trying to pin every case you can't solve on this so-called Iceman." Wilson snorted. "Biggest drug dealer in the Bay area, right, Jack? Except we don't have prints, we don't have a description. . . . You're about the only cop on the force who even believes this guy exists!"

Jack balled his fists inside his coat pockets and thought about how much he hated guys like Wilson, men who couldn't see past the nose on their face. Wilson wasn't interested unless all the facts fit together. But sometimes one had to follow one's hunches and use one's imagination to get the big picture. Jack was willing to bet his pension that he was on the trail of a *very* big picture.

"I'm gonna let you in on a little secret, Cates. There is no Iceman," said Wilson, his face turning red with anger. "So let's get back to the cold facts of this case—because *this* is real. What the hell happened here?"

"I saw an exchange. Probable cause. I moved in. He had a piece. He shot, I shot back," Cates curtly explained.

Wilson looked bored. *If it were really that simple,* he thought. "You got the bad guy's gun?"

Cates shook his head. "I didn't touch anything. It's gotta be in there with the ashes and shit."

"Then you got no problem. As long as they find the gun . . ." he said, looking at the other officers still poking through the cinders.

"What you got, Cruise?" demanded Wilson.

Cruise stared at his blackened hands and took a

while answering. "Nothin', just some burned metal. Must be off the pump."

"No gun?"

"No," Cruise admitted reluctantly. "No gun."

Wilson wore a poker face when he turned back to Cates. "You know what I think, Jack?"

"Yeah, I got a pretty good fuckin' idea," Cates said grudgingly.

"I think you were going along, thinking you were doing your job, and you stepped on your dick," said Wilson, lighting another cigarette. "That sound right? Look, a cop is a guy. A guy sometimes steps on his dick. You think maybe today you were pushing a little too hard, trying to make something work, and you stepped on your dick? Work with me here, Cates! We're on the same side. Did you step on your dick?"

Pleased with himself for having presented Cates with an out, Wilson lit another cigarette and waited smugly for Cates to accept the bait.

Jack wasn't biting. Not today . . . not ever. The bad guy was for real, and the only cop who was pushing too hard was Wilson. He could take his dumb-ass theory and shove it.

"Goddammit! It didn't go down that way. He had a piece," Jack said stubbornly. "He shot. I shot back."

Wilson's smile faded. "I want the lab boys to go over every inch of this place," he snapped at Kehoe. "If there was a gun, I want it. A bullet. Something. Anything."

He'd done what he could for Cates, but the poor slob had a death wish. Cates was a headstrong fool—the most dangerous kind there was. Everyone knew he had more enemies than friends in the department. With his track record, it wouldn't take much to bring him up on charges that would put him permanently out of harm's way.

He whirled around and bared his teeth in what was supposed to be a smile. "See ya around, Cates."

Jack was as sure as he was alive that the dead mechanic had pulled a gun on him. But the damned thing seemed to have vanished among the smoldering ashes of the gas-pump explosion. Following Wilson's orders—and because no cop liked to see another cop proved a liar—a team of San Francisco's finest spent hours painstakingly combing through the hay and rubble. For their trouble, they found nothing but a handful of used condoms, a rusted switchblade, some spare bike parts, and a nest of field mice.

No gun. No bullet. *Nada.* Not a single shred of evidence to support Cates's claim of self-defense.

Barely masking his glee, Wilson wasted no time presenting his case against Cates to the Police Review Board. It took only a few days for the board members to examine the file and summon those concerned to a hearing at police headquarters.

For once Cates did as he was told and brought his lawyer, Harry Bryant, to the small, sparsely furnished hearing room. Wilson was there, of course, seated at the other end of the large rectangular conference table that dominated the room. He was flanked by his pretty, young female assistant, who scribbled notes throughout the proceedings. Kehoe, Cruise, and a couple of uniformed officers who'd been present at the racetrack were also seated around the table, on hand to testify and lend Cates their moral support.

Kehoe and Cruise, in particular, did their best to slant their testimony in Cates's favor. But the six board members, two of them civilians, asked difficult, pointed questions that left Harry Bryant looking grim.

His client radiated unadulterated fury. Listening to Wilson describe what *he'd* seen that morning at the track, Jack narrowed his green eyes and set his thin lips tightly, as if he were afraid of what might come out if he opened his mouth. Though he managed to keep his mouth shut, he couldn't control his body language. He squirmed and twisted and shifted in his seat, until Bryant finally hissed in his ear, "Can't you sit still for five minutes?"

"Screw you!" Jack growled sotto voce. But he hunkered down in his chair and confined his reaction to a poorly concealed scowl.

A brief recess was called toward the middle of the afternoon. In less time than it should have taken to reach a decision, the board sent word that it was ready to reconvene. They were already seated when the rest of the participants filed in and took their places.

The chairman, a white-haired gentleman who looked as if he hadn't seen the inside of a station house in too many years to understand what made a good cop, cleared his throat and leaned forward.

"In the matter of the officer-involved shooting at Hunter's Point Raceway of the suspect, Arthur Brock, a resident of San Francisco," he addressed the group, avoiding Cates's stare. "The review board has carefully examined the physical evidence and the testimony of the witnesses, and has determined that the officer in question, Inspector Jack Cates, had insufficient probable cause. Based on a review of the officer's case history, and an ongoing investigation by the Internal

Affairs Division, this review board cannot help but rule that the shooting was a wrongful action."

Jack's shaggy blond hair fell over his eyes as he shook his head disbelievingly. His mouth formed the words, but didn't say aloud, *son-of-a-bitch*. When Bryant reached over and touched his arm by way of consolation, Jack jerked away, needing to be left alone in his misery.

A buzz of shock filled the room. Frank Cruise slapped his palm against the wooden tabletop and demanded of Kehoe, who was seated next to him, "Why the hell's Wilson coming down on Jack so hard?"

"He hates him. Has for years," Kehoe told him. "Jack got loaded one night and told him that he and everybody in his division were complete chicken-shits."

"Jack's right! Cops aren't supposed to rat on each other. We should take all these Internal Affairs guys and shoot 'em in the legs. Blow out their kneecaps," Cruise declared indignantly.

Bryant began stuffing his papers into his briefcase. "I really didn't think they'd land this heavy on you," he told his client.

Just then, Wilson stopped by Cates's table on his way out. "Look, Jack, I'm sorry," he apologized, "but I'm afraid I'm going to have to recommend to the district attorney that he prosecute for manslaughter. I really wish they'd found a gun. Sorry, Jack," he said again. "I'm just doing my job. Good luck."

Cates glowered as Wilson brushed past but kept his comments to himself. Ignoring the No Smoking signs that were posted around the room, he pulled out his cigarettes and lit up.

"Wilson's got a personality profile of an obsessed cop whose record shows his history of stepping over the line," said Bryant, batting away the smoke. "It's quite likely the D.A. will choose to prosecute you on third-degree."

"In other words," Kehoe threw in his two cents, "you're screwed."

"Unless I can find the Iceman," Jack tossed back at him.

"C'mon, Jack, give it up," urged Kehoe. "That's what got you into this—"

Cates stared at him incredulously. "You sound like Wilson, Ben. For Chrissakes, you want me to forget about this guy? Let him go loose? Or do you think I'm ready for the rubber-gun squad?"

His chair scraped against the floor as he stood up to leave. Grabbing his raincoat, he stormed out of the room without so much as a good-bye.

Kehoe hurried after him. "Hey, I'm on your side. I wanna help," he objected heatedly, struggling to keep up with Cates. "But we're talking about the facts here. You got no leads, the department's got no leads . . . this is manslaughter! Protect yourself!"

His words echoed hollowly as they followed Jack down the spiral staircase. But they fell on deaf ears. Taking the steps two at a time, Jack was listening to his inner voice. He didn't give a shit what leads the department did or didn't have. The department could go screw itself ten times over. For damn sure it had already screwed him.

Jack had his own set of facts. With any luck, it would lead him to the Iceman.

• 4

"You must be a real dangerous convict!" yelled Cates.

He was standing in the middle of an open-roofed prison exercise space the size of a football field. The room, which was surrounded by hundred-foot-high walls, was empty except for a bustle of activity at the far end. Four guards were stationed at each corner of the basketball court, their pump shotguns trained on the lone prisoner who was shooting baskets from the foul line.

His voice boomed out across the yard just as the prisoner was taking aim at the basket. The ball lofted upward, took a slight dip as it sailed toward the basket, and wavered just above the rim before it bounced heavily against the backboard.

Reggie Hammond shook his head in disgust as he turned to acknowledge Cates. "Look what you did, cop. You made me miss," he said, bending to retrieve the basketball.

Taking care to avoid the pigeon droppings that speckled the surface of the gym floor, he dribbled the ball across the court until he was within spitting distance of Jack Cates.

"Hey, Reggie!" Jack greeted him enthusiastically. "You look good."

Reggie put his hands on his hips and regarded the cop with grave skepticism. It wasn't like Cates to be handing out compliments. Otherwise, not much else had changed. He still sounded as if he gargled with gravel every morning, and his tweed jacket could have come out of a Salvation Army bin. And he still had a whole lot of goddamned nerve, dropping by just as Reggie was about to be let out.

"First time you dragged your ass down here in five years," Reggie reminded him, recalling the last time Cates showed up, back before Reggie had been transferred from San Quentin to Folsom. Cates had wanted Reggie's help in tracking down two guys who'd killed a couple of his cop buddies. "Up yours," Reggie told him, figuring it was none of his business—until Cates mentioned that Albert Ganz had busted out of jail.

Suddenly it became very much Reggie's business. He and Ganz had briefly run with the same gang. In the course of committing armed robbery, they had happened upon a drug deal involving a large chunk of change—"the kind of money nobody reports stolen" was how Reggie had explained it to Cates. Reggie had walked away with an even half-million.

Reggie figured his share was safe while he was in prison because Ganz's sentence was two years longer than his. But with Ganz on the loose, the money was in serious danger of winding up in Ganz's hands.

Reggie and Cates had spent only forty-eight hours together—but what a forty-eight hours it had been. Reggie quickly discovered that Jack Cates was an evil-tempered, booze-swigging cop who never hesitated to play rough. He could be a real asshole, but he was a *fair* asshole who didn't give up when the cause was important enough. During those two memorable days, they'd chased Ganz and his pal Billy Bear all over San Francisco. They'd ultimately blown their brains out in a winner-takes-all gunfight.

By then, Reggie and Cates had grudgingly come to trust and even almost like each other. In fact, Reggie had trusted Jack enough to leave his stash with him. He'd also expected the guy to pay him a visit once in a while. But this was the first he'd seen of Jack since Cates had escorted him back to San Quentin at the end of his two-day furlough.

Reggie was pissed at Cates, and he wanted the bastard to know it. "I thought you was my friend," he told the cop, giving the basketball a couple of bounces.

"Aw, look, I'm sorry. I been busy," Jack defended himself.

"Me, too," Reggie said coldly. "What do you want, Jack?" he asked, not yet ready to forgive Cates. "Must be real pressing if you waited all this time. You even got a haircut."

"Times change," said Cates, sucking on a cigarette.

"You lost weight."

"Quit drinkin'."

"So what *do* you want?" Reggie demanded, fed up with whatever game Cates was playing. "They send you up here to tell me my sentence is being jacked up again?"

"Relax," grumbled Cates. Somehow the conversation wasn't going the way he'd anticipated.

"You're still gettin' out tomorrow," he assured Hammond. "But when you do, you and me's gotta do another little job. . . ."

Reggie was shaking his head before Cates finished making his speech. "There's nothing you and me gotta do when I get out. I did your dirty work once before and all it got me was jackshit. All you gotta do is give me back my money and I'm gone. Out of town. Out of sight. *Gone.*"

He stared defiantly at Cates, who wasn't the least bit impressed by his speech. "You don't get it, Reggie," he said, all traces of warmth suddenly gone from his voice. "You help me out of this one—or you're not gettin' your money back."

Another man might have been intimidated by Cates's threat. Not Reggie Hammond. He knew how tough Cates could be, but Reggie could be every bit as tough.

"I gave you that money for safekeeping. You said that money would be waiting for me. Now you're telling me you're not gonna give it back?" he challenged Cates.

"That's right, convict," Cates said as enthusiastically as a game-show host telling a contestant that he'd just won the jackpot.

Reggie exploded with five years' worth of pent-up resentment. With one fluid motion, he stiff-armed the basketball and smashed it into Cates's face, hitting him square in the mouth. Cates staggered backward, struggling to maintain his balance. Taking advantage of the moment, Reggie threw a sharp right uppercut that caught Cates in the gut and blasted the wind out of him.

Jack grunted and doubled over in pain. The guards rushed forward and grabbed their prisoner, pinning his arms behind his back. Jack straightened up slowly and stared malevolently at Hammond. Reggie knew he was in for it now, but he had no regrets. He'd waited a long time to lay that on Cates.

But Cates surprised him. Waving the guards away, he growled, "Let him go!" He checked his mouth for damage, then hiked up his pants and turned to leave. "I'll give you that one, Reggie," he said over his shoulder. "On account."

"On account of you fucking me up!" Reggie yelled at Cates's retreating back. Feeling as if he'd been there before, Reggie shouted, "Where you going? Come back! Cates!"

Cates lit up a cigarette and kept right on walking.

"I'm coming out tomorrow, Cates! I waited five years for that fucking money! I want my fucking money! Cates!" Reggie screamed, a note of desperation creeping into his voice. "Cates!"

Cates could still hear Reggie screaming his name as the guard unlocked the door that led to the main reception area. Under the circumstances, their reunion had gone very well, Cates thought. He would sleep well tonight, knowing he had Reggie Hammond exactly where he wanted him.

Hickok, Price, and Cherry roared into San Francisco as if they owned the town and drove straight over to Barnstormers, a seedy downtown bar south of Market near the Embarcadero. At night, the bar's walls shook from the pounding beat of the music, and a person could hardly hear himself think. But this early in the day, the place was deserted except for a few working stiffs who needed a belt or two to hold them until lunch.

The bartender, Terry, was a pretty, bleached-blond woman in her early twenties. She hated working the graveyard shift because the sad-faced drunks sobbing into their beers about their lost wives and jobs were notoriously poor tippers. So when the three mean-eyed dudes covered with dust from the road strolled through the door, she pasted on a smile and tried to look friendly.

"Bottle of tequila," ordered Price, slapping a twenty under her nose.

Hickok moved in on her next. "Whiskey," he demanded, checking her out from behind his shades.

"And?" she asked.

"And put it in a glass." He grinned and poked Cherry in the ribs.

"Cute," said Terry, cracking her gum.

Price worked his way down to the far end of the bar where Burroughs was waiting for him.

"Mr. Price," Burroughs said quietly.

"Tequila?" offered Price, holding up the bottle.

Burroughs nodded. "Thanks."

He watched in silence as Price poured him a generous glassful. Then he tossed back a healthy swig—it went down easy after the morning's fiasco at the racetrack—and broke the bad news to Price. "The Man's distressed. The mess you made in the desert has him wondering if your boys are going to be around to finish the job."

"Not to worry," said Price, refilling both glasses. He'd been expecting this message, and he had a message of his own for Burroughs's boss. "These two get on a fella's case, the fella dies."

Burroughs grimaced. "Real pros, huh? Not from where I'm sitting. Pros don't make messes like you did. Don't have the heat jacked up when they're supposed to be doing a job."

Emboldened by the tequila, Price didn't care who Burroughs was working for. "You're pitiful," he declared, angrily spitting out the words. "You wanna be an outlaw, but you wanna play by rules. There are no rules. There's only the condition your condition is in."

"You giving me your philosophy, man?" Burroughs asked, a scornful smile playing around his lips.

"Sure. We're the only real Americans left. We believe in freedom. That's why people are scared of us," Price informed him, warming to his subject. "'Cause we do what everyone else is too chickenshit to do. We live the way folks used to, back before there were big cities and lawyers and computers with your name in 'em. Free. The rest of you"—Price gestured wildly—"you're just a bunch o' slaves."

"Yeah?" Burroughs sneered, wishing he could shove his fist in Price's ugly face. "Well, that's real interesting, Mr. Price. *Real* interesting. Maybe you should run for office. All I'm supposed to tell you is that the Man wants you to take precautions. We tried to hire some backup for you, but he got deep-fried out at a race track."

From under the table, Burroughs produced a small nylon bag and held it open for Price to examine. "You know what to do with that stuff?"

Price checked the contents of the bag. "No problem here, friend. I used to be a Marine." He smiled.

"I guess that figures." Burroughs replied. "You got a problem, you guys come to me. Just call the number."

While Price was taking the heat from Burroughs, his partners were busy getting loaded. At about the same moment that Price was going on about what was wrong with America, Cherry was finishing off his second whiskey.

"Another," he announced, leering at Terry's amply proportioned breasts, which threatened to spill out of her tight halter top.

He gulped the third down even faster than the first two and licked up the tiny drops of whiskey that clung to the ends of his moustache. Then he jerked Terry closer and whispered something in her ear.

Terry's smile faded fast. "I think you got the wrong girl. I don't do that," she said, pulling away from him.

"C'mon, we just hit town. I'm lookin' for a little whore who works here," said Cherry, as Hickok watched with amusement.

"Oh, yeah? What's her name?" Terry asked suspiciously, rearranging her top.

"Angel."

"Angel don't work here anymore. She's dancin' up in North Beach."

"But you're here," Cherry pointed out. He leaned across the bar and grabbed at her breasts. "How much for a look at those?"

"I'm getting sick of this, buddy," Terry fumed, edging away from him once more.

"Anything you think is reasonable, honey. Just a cheap fuck," Cherry coaxed as he reached for her again.

"Cut it out!" she said angrily.

Hickok sidled closer so that she was trapped between them behind the bar. Trying not to let her panic show, she lied, "Look, mister, I'm married."

"So was my mother," cracked Cherry. "It never stopped her."

He and Hickok doubled over, howling with laughter.

Finally Cherry stopped guffawing long enough to say, "C'mon. I promised my friend a good time."

"Well, then *you* go fuck him," Terry snapped.

It took a second for her comment to sink into Cherry's whiskey-sotted brain. Then, his face contorted with rage, he lunged forward, grabbed hold of her skimpy top, and pulled her toward him.

"Let go!" Terry yelled. "I'll call the police—"

Hickok slammed his gun down on top of the bar. "Go ahead, sweet cheeks. Call 'em." He flashed her a smile that glittered with menace.

Cherry was just beginning to enjoy himself when suddenly Price broke in on them. "Let's hit the road, boys," he said.

Hickok shrugged and picked up his gun. "Forget the bitch, Cherry."

But Cherry wasn't about to give up so easily. "I'm just gonna tear me off some—"

"I *said,*" exploded Hickok, throwing a hard punch to his shoulder, "forget the bitch!"

Cherry let go of Terry and grabbed for Hickok's shirt, looking as if he were about to rip him in half. But Hickok coolly stared his pal down, until Cherry finally relaxed his grip.

That was exactly what Price had been worried about. Cherry was a hotheaded fool who'd just handed Burroughs another reason to doubt their ability to finish the job.

As if to hammer home the point, Cherry whirled around and caught Burroughs staring at him. "What're you looking at?" he snarled.

"Cool it, boys," barked Price. "He works for the Man."

Burroughs had seen and heard enough. Maybe these were the right men for the job, or maybe not. As long as he didn't get caught in the crossfire, he didn't give a shit who ended up eating a bullet. He picked up his raincoat, nodded briskly at Price, and said, "You got a problem, you come to me. Just call the number."

He left without saying good-bye.

But Cherry, as usual, had to have the last word. He cocked his index finger at Terry and pretended to take aim. "You're lucky," he told her.

She was more than willing to take his word for it.

5

Reggie didn't need a whole lot of time to pack for his trip back to freedom. He left behind his toothbrush, a couple of paperbacks he'd reread so often that they were falling apart, and the *Penthouse* pictures with which he'd decorated the walls of his cell. All he took with him was his Walkman, which had seen him through more lonely days and nights than he cared to count. He was ready and waiting when two guards arrived to escort him out of the cellblock.

"Let's go," said one of them.

Reggie didn't have to be asked twice.

Freedom! For years he'd thought and dreamed of nothing else: the freedom to feel a woman's soft skin against his flesh . . . to indulge himself in expensive wines and five-course dinners in candlelit restaurants . . . to buy himself a brand-new thousand-dollar suit,

. . . to fit his hands around the wheel of his Porsche, put his foot on the gas, and take off in any direction that suited his fancy.

Freedom was a flavor that came in countless different tastes and smells, and he damned well intended to try out every last one of them. He was lucky to have the money to do just that. No, Reggie corrected himself. It wasn't a matter of luck. It was a matter of his being one smart dude who'd happened to be in the right place at the right time.

Of course, the first thing he had to do was get his money back from Cates. He didn't give a damn what little job Cates had in mind for them to do together. That screwed-up cop had proved that he was no friend of Reggie's. He ought to know better than to expect favors. Reggie Hammond's name was written all over that money. He'd earned it the hard way, sitting on his butt all these years in jail.

Now, headed in the direction of freedom, he took one last look around him. As he passed by their cells, the other inmates called out good-natured insults and gibes. "Don't forget to write!" shouted one.

"Don't worry, you'll be back before you know it," promised another.

"You get yourself some pussy on me, ya hear?" shouted a third.

"Reggie!" One voice rang out above the others.

Reggie wiped the smile off his face and stopped dead in his tracks. Staring at him through the steel bars was Kirkland Smith, a grizzled, square-jawed black man with a powerful build and a reputation for being mean and ornery.

"You didn't forget your promise, Reggie, right?"

thundered Kirkland. "I just want to hear you say it. . . ."

Reggie stepped closer to Kirkland's cell and said in his most conciliatory tone, "Sure, no problem, man."

He didn't need any overdue notices to remind him of his debt to Kirkland, which he intended to repay as soon as possible. The name of the game was staying *alive.* But you didn't stand much of a chance if you crossed the line and found yourself on the wrong side of Kirkland Smith.

"That big white cop come to see you the other night isn't gonna screw anything up, is he?" Kirkland demanded suspiciously.

"No. No way." Reggie tried to stay cool as he sought to reassure the con. "I mean, it might take a little longer than I thought—"

"I don't want any bullshit." Kirkland cut short Reggie's explanation. "You get that money. And you keep your word. I kept you alive for the last five years. Lemme tell you somethin' else, jiveass. I can get you out there. I can see to it that your neck gets broke. Don't forget it."

"Hey! I like breathin' too much to break my word to you. That's the truth," Reggie said, defending himself.

He didn't have time to say more before the guards hustled him out of the cellblock. As they led him past the machine shops, truck docks, and car sidings that made up the prison work area, Reggie took one last look around and swore to himself that he'd never be back. He'd learned his lesson. No more guns. No more bad company. No more trouble. Half a million dollars said that starting today, he was going straight and keeping his ass out of jail.

Just past the work area was the main building, where his exit papers would be processed for check-out. The warden was already there, waiting for him, next to a wire-veined window behind which stood a uniformed clerk.

Above the window was a sign that read STAND ON THE LINE. Reggie's heart was singing as he stepped forward and carefully planted his feet along the designated spot.

"Hammond, Reggie A.," said the guard, sliding Reggie's papers through the slit in the window. The clerk took the papers and went off to find Reggie's belongings, impounded when he'd first arrived at the prison.

Reggie flashed a broad grin at the warden. "Come on, let's have it. I actually want to hear it."

The warden couldn't wait to see the last of Hammond. "What?" he asked.

"The speech about me screwing up and coming right back. How you'll keep my cell warm, how you seen 'em come and you seen 'em go. I been waiting seven years to hear that speech. Wouldn't feel right to leave without it."

"I was just going to say you get a hundred dollars and a free bus ride to San Francisco—all courtesy of the state of California," the warden curtly informed him. He handed Reggie a white envelope and shook his hand.

Not much a man can do with five twenties, Reggie thought. But he decided to keep the money, on principle. It was the least the state of California owed him.

The clerk reappeared behind the mesh-covered window. "Hammond, Reggie A. Here you go," he announced, passing Reggie a thick manila envelope and a package wrapped in brown butcher's paper.

Reggie blew a thick layer of dust off the envelope, opened it up, and inspected its contents: a gold, square-cut pinky ring, his Rolex wristwatch, and his wallet.

"Hey!" he exclaimed. "Where's my James Brown tape? When I came in here, I had a James Brown tape."

"It's in there," said the bored clerk.

Reggie reached into the bottom of the envelope and came up with the missing tape. "Good. Everybody's tryin' to keep James in prison," he said with an impish grin.

Satisfied that all his personal possessions had been returned to him, he turned next to the package and ripped open the paper—his civilian threads . . . and what a set of threads they were! His grin broadened as he held the suit up against himself.

Reggie Hammond couldn't wait to hit the street!

Dressed in the same Armani suit he'd worn into prison, Reggie was still smiling when he strolled through the metal door just inside the main gate. But his face went flat when he noticed who was slouched against the wall, waiting for him.

"I don't think we got to finish our conversation," said Cates, grinding a cigarette butt beneath the toe of his boot.

"Get out of here." Reggie dismissed him and kept right on walking. "We got nothin' to talk about until I get my money."

"Told you yesterday. You're not gettin' it unless you help me," Cates calmly replied.

Reggie stopped walking and pointed an accusing finger at Cates. "I don't believe this. I trusted you with my money *and* my Porsche because I thought you were straight. What the fuck is going on?"

Pleased that he'd finally caught Reggie's attention, Jack said, "I been chasing a drug dealer called the Iceman for four years. Last week I find out he wants you dead." He pulled Reggie's picture out of his pocket and held it up for Reggie to see. "Got this off a guy paying someone to make a hit on you. That makes you the best lead I've ever had."

Reggie stared at Cates as if the cop had lost his marbles. Did he expect Hammond to believe that story? Yeah, sure. *When hell froze over.* "Helping you out, when you're keepin' my money, is the last thing I want to do," he spat.

As if on cue, the big iron gate swung open and Reggie stepped through to the other side, a free man. But Cates was right there by his side. "I'm just tryin' to keep you alive, Reggie," he said, sounding hurt.

"I kept myself alive in here for five years. I don't need your help," Reggie shot back, tired of the man's jive. He looked up the road and spotted his ride back to the real world. A gray-and-black bus with the words CALIFORNIA DEPARTMENT OF CORRECTIONS stenciled on the side was parked a few yards to his right.

Reggie hurried for the bus, shouting at Cates, "Leave me to rot in prison for five years and then expect me to help you! That's bullshit! That's worse than bullshit—that's dumb!"

"No, Reggie, wait. Wait!" Cates grabbed Reggie's arm, forcing him to stop walking. "I promise you, this time it's gonna be different. I don't just lose my badge . . ." He took a deep breath and finally admitted the depths of his desperation. "I go to jail."

"Oh, your ass in trouble with the law?" Reggie hooted, pulling his arm away. He was really starting to enjoy the sound of Cates singing the blues. "Good. *Good!* Bad as I feel about you keepin' my money, that almost makes up for it. Now I'm *sure* I don't want to help you."

"I don't beg . . . so don't push me, fucker!" Cates blustered.

Reggie laughed aloud. "What're you gonna do? Shoot me? Beat the shit outta me right here in front of the prison? That's not a real smart way to handle the best lead you've ever had."

Reggie took a deep breath and filled his lungs with the smell of fresh air. Then he turned to take one last look at the imposing stone walls that surrounded the prison. His field of vision was disturbed, however, by the miserable expression on Cates's face, which even he couldn't manage to disguise.

"Don't worry, Jack. I'll come back here in five or six years and visit you," he said jauntily.

He hopped aboard the bus, threw Cates a brief salute, and told the bus driver, "All right. Let's go."

"Couple of minutes," said the driver, a beefy-faced man named Dick Reilly, who was dressed in the uniform of the state correction system.

Reggie glared at the driver. "What?"

"Schedule. Couple of minutes before we take off."

"This is my time, man, not the state's," argued Reggie, impatient to be on his way back to civilization.

Reilly, who didn't take orders from ex-cons,

grunted and said, "Write a letter." And he double-checked his watch. He hunkered down in his seat and closed his eyes. Nobody was going anywhere until he was good and ready.

"It's Christmas!" shouted Cherry, catching sight of Cates through the lenses of his high-powered binoculars.

He and Hickok were sitting astride their idling bikes, parked on a hill overlooking the front of the prison.

He handed the binoculars to Hickok and said, "The big fucker in the blue Caddy . . ." He waited for Hickok to focus. "That's the pig who wasted my brother. This is great. I get both of 'em."

Hickok lowered the glasses and shook his head dubiously. "The Iceman didn't say anything about a cop."

"The pig wasted my family," Cherry reminded him, stashing the binoculars in their case, then adjusting his sunglasses.

Hickok pulled his sunglasses down over his eyes. "I thought you never much liked your brother."

"It's the principle, man," Cherry explained, sounding as if he were teaching a civics lesson. "Somebody kills your brother, you're supposed to do something about it."

Hickok nodded. He got the picture. The two men gunned their engines, popped their Harleys into wheelies, and shot off down the hill.

"Oh, yeah!" shrieked Cherry above the roar of his bike and the rush of the wind. "Oh, yeah!"

* * *

U.S. 50 was a thin, gray ribbon of a road that wound between the gently rolling hills of California's fertile Central Valley. It didn't often see much traffic—let alone a car like Cates's baby-blue Cadillac convertible. With its long fins and fifties-style, wide-bodied grille, the Caddy was a far cry from the utilitarian cars and tractors that normally traveled back and forth along the two-lane highway.

Never mind that the sides were streaked with mud, that the windshield was splattered with dead insects, or that the shocks were shot to hell. Five years earlier, chasing down Albert Ganz and Billy Bear, Cates had driven a baby blue Caddy just like this one through a plate-glass window. The car had been wrecked beyond repair. It had taken him six months to find another.

This sweet ragtop baby had a hold on Cates's heart like no woman ever could. Few things in life could compare with the pleasure of speeding down an empty highway with the top down and the wind whipping through his hair.

Jack believed that speed limits were made to be broken, and he'd gotten a good head start on Reggie's bus. His stomach was rumbling with hunger, so he decided to grab a quick bite at the diner just up ahead on his right. He pulled off the highway and slammed on the brakes, creating a cloud of dust that he brought inside with him when he pushed open the door.

The place was a clean, cheerful luncheonette, decorated with brass candlesticks, china roosters, and lacy valances hung across the tops of the windows. Though it was a big step up from the greasy spoons and candy machines where he usually ate his meals, Jack hardly noticed the decor.

He took a seat at the counter, spread out a bundle of files marked PROPERTY OF SAN FRANCISCO POLICE DEPARTMENT, and pulled on his reading glasses to consult the menu. This was a working breakfast.

A heavyset waitress dropped a napkin and table setting in front of him. Order pad in hand, she said, "What can I do you for this morning, mister?"

"You got any food left?" Cates needled her.

"Plenty," answered the waitress, who'd heard it all before.

"Give me corned-beef hash with three eggs over easy," Cates told her, glancing again at the menu, "a hard roll, coffee, and a side of bacon."

The waitress nodded and started toward the kitchen.

"Not finished," he grunted. "I also want a short stack, and biscuits with gravy."

"You missed a few things on the other side of the menu," joked the waitress, pouring him a cup of coffee.

Jack didn't bother responding. He'd already stuck his nose inside the top file and was absentmindedly ruining his coffee with too much sugar. A minute later, he looked up in time to see the prison bus go roaring past. What he didn't notice were the two bikers riding right behind the bus. Nor did he see them pull off the road and slow to a stop next to his Caddy.

Absorbed in his reading, Cates slowly became aware of a sharp rapping noise. He swiveled around in his stool and peered over the top of his glasses. Framed in the glass was a vaguely familiar-looking man who was apparently tapping on the window to get his attention.

Judging by his getup, Cates figured him to be a

biker. The man's eyes were hidden behind wraparound shades, but his smile seemed friendly and his left hand waved a greeting. Cates was still puzzling over how he knew the biker when the man suddenly raised his right hand. He was holding a shiny chrome .44 Magnum—and it was aimed at Cates's head.

Cates reached inside his jacket for his gun. But he was a crucial second behind Cherry, who aimed and blasted eight bullets through the window. Cates ducked, but his timing was off by a second. He yelped with shock and pain as six bullets slammed into his chest, catapulting him backward over the counter.

As he tumbled to the floor, gasping for breath, two more bullets slammed against the mirrored wall behind the counter. The waitress, who'd just walked out of the kitchen, screamed as the glass exploded. Her trayful of food went flying, and she flopped to the floor, shrieking with terror.

Cherry gleefully surveyed the damage he'd wrought at the diner in just two short minutes. Satisfied that he'd done his bit to avenge his brother's death, he waved again, *bye-bye, asshole.* Then he happily retraced his steps up to the road, where Hickok was waiting for him. He quickly replaced the spent magazine in his automatic for a fully loaded one. Then he signaled to Hickok that he was ready to ride. It was time to earn some money. They roared back on to the main road, in search of Reggie Hammond.

But Cherry had underestimated his enemy. Jack Cates was down, but he was far from dead. While the hysterical waitress looked on in helpless, frozen horror, Jack struggled to raise himself to his knees. Dazed and hurting badly, he drew on his deep reserves of stubborn determination to stay alive. One thought kept him going: He had to get to his gun in case the biker returned.

Operating purely on animal instinct, he focused on survival. Blood seeped through his shirt as he dragged himself, inch by agonizing inch, toward his gun.

Cates had been shot before, but this pain was different from anything he'd ever experienced. This pain was so piercing, so all-consuming, that he could hardly breathe from the shock of it. Crawling across the floor, he felt as if he were battling a dense, white mist that at any moment threatened to close in and swallow him up.

By the time his hand touched the cold steel of his gun, he'd used up everything he had left in him. The mist was rolling in fast and thick when his trembling fingers slowly closed around the butt. He tried to stand, couldn't summon the energy, fell back to the floor. The waitress stumbled toward him to give him a hand, but she was too late. Jack was already unconscious.

• 6

Reggie hadn't even gotten where he wanted to go, and already he was having himself a *good* time. He stared through the bus's exhaust-streaked windows at the green grass swaying in the wind, and thought about an old girlfriend who'd always smelled as fresh as summer. Maybe he'd look her up again one of these days. It sure had been a while. . . .

To his right in the caged-off area behind the driver's seat sat two handcuffed cons complaining loudly about the lack of air conditioning on the bus. They'd been carrying on since the first moment they'd been put aboard. Reggie had heard about as much as he could take of their bellyaching. He pulled out his Walkman, slipped on the headphones, and pressed the Play button.

The space between his ears was filled with the

incomparable voice of James Brown singing "Ow! I got the feeling, baby! Ow! . . ."

Reggie sang right along, matching James note for note.

The cons tried to shut him up by rattling their handcuffs in his direction. The driver tried to shut him out by keeping his eyes on the road. Through his sideview mirror, Reilly caught a glimpse of two bikers making the turn onto the highway from an access road. He crested a hill and downshifted from second to first. The road behind him dipped, and the bikers seemed to vanish.

A half-mile farther, he rechecked the sideview and still couldn't find them. He blinked and looked again. He was sure he'd seen two guys dressed in black leather riding monster cycles. Could he have imagined it? *Naw,* he told himself. *They must have changed their minds and turned around.* Or maybe they'd slipped over onto the shoulder while he was concentrating on the road ahead of him.

Reilly hadn't lost the bikers. Cherry and Hickok were just having a little fun with him. They'd pulled up right behind the bus, tailing him so closely that they weren't visible in either the sideview or the rearview mirror. But now it was time to stop playing and get to work. Hickok suddenly accelerated into the oncoming traffic lane. Riding parallel with the bus, he craned his neck and checked each window as he moved toward the front.

Where the hell was Hammond?

He sped up, still riding on the wrong side of the road, and almost collided head-on with a motor home. The motor home swerved and barely missed hitting the bus.

"Dumb shits!" Reilly cursed the biker, and suddenly there were two of them in front of the bus.

The driver leaned hard on his horn as the bikers slowed and began to weave back and forth ahead of him.

"Stupid idiots!" yelled Reilly, repeatedly honking his horn at them.

The blaring horn was music to Hickok's ears. It only confirmed what he already knew—that he was king of the road. Whooping with the joy of the chase, he whipped across the highway and positioned himself so that he could check the windows on the right side of the bus. He'd almost reached the back when he finally found what he'd been looking for.

"Baby-baby-baby-baby-ow! Baby—" Reggie harmonized with James.

He was so wrapped up in the music that it took a couple of seconds before he noticed the biker riding abreast of his window. Their eyes met. Hickok smiled and greeted Reggie with an upraised arm, as if he were hailing an old friend.

Reggie gave him a tentative smile. Who was this dude who was acting as if he knew him? There'd been plenty of bikers in jail. But they didn't much like the brothers, and he'd kept his distance from them.

With one hand on his handlebar, Hickok reached with the other into his bedroll. Out came a drum-fed shotgun. Hickok leveled the gun at Reggie's eyes and prayed for a bull's-eye. He pulled the trigger—

Boom!

The bullet crashed through the glass and whistled past the empty space where Reggie's head had been a scant millisecond earlier.

"Get down! Stay down!" screamed Reilly.

Reggie was way ahead of him. That mother was using a *serious* gun. Reggie had a healthy respect for automatic weapons, especially when they were aimed at his head. While the handcuffed cons screamed and Reilly fed the gas, Reggie scrambled up the aisle on his hands and knees, trying to escape the rifle fire. But Hickok kept coming after him, his shotgun blazing, methodically blowing out every window on the right side of the bus.

Desperate to ditch the biker, Reilly veered into the opposite lane and narrowly missed hitting a pickup truck. Zigzagging back into his own lane, he yelled frantically into his radio, "Come in, C.H.P. Central twenty-one-twenty, this is Dick Reilly in Folsom Prison transport number six. I'm heading west on U.S. Highway Fifty! I'm being attacked by bikers! They have guns! The bus is being attacked! Get some help over here right away! I need help!"

Double-ought pellets ripped through the side of the bus. Reilly tried to steer to the right. Suddenly his eyes widened with terror. The second biker, riding directly in front of the bus, was standing up in his seat, pointing a gun over his shoulder.

Unlike Reggie, Dick Reilly didn't have time to duck.

Cherry fired his .44 once . . . twice . . .

The first shot caught Reilly on the side of the neck and severed his carotid artery. He bounced off the wire screen behind his seat. The second bullet hit him in the forehead and got lodged in his brain. He slumped forward, dead almost before he knew what had hit him.

The driverless bus lurched across the highway dividing line like a drunken elephant. Keeping his head low, Reggie half-crawled, half-stumbled to the front of the bus and pushed aside the driver's body. Grabbing hold of the blood-slicked steering wheel, he angled it sharply to the right. The bus fishtailed right. Its back end bounced Hickok off the road and onto the shoulder.

Yanking the wheel to the left, Reggie fought to steer the bus back onto the highway. He glanced through the shattered windshield and yelped with surprise. He hit the floor at the same instant that a bullet from Cherry's .44 Magnum blew out what was left of the windshield.

The driverless bus careened across both lanes and rocked out of control, tilting dangerously to one side. The two right tires shuddered from the weight overload, then exploded with a bone-bruising *whoomph!* The bus jolted crazily across the highway, then rolled sideways into the path of a tractor-trailer truck that was just cresting the hill.

The truck driver twisted his wheel, slammed on his brakes, and did what he could to avoid the bus. But he was fighting a losing battle. His cab plowed into the back end of the bus. The trailer jackknifed, and the chains that held in place his load of irrigation pipes burst under the impact. Row after row of enormous steel cylinders came crashing off the flatbed and thundered across the grassy meadows on either side of the highway.

Dazed and shaken, Reggie struggled to free himself from where he lay pinned behind the metal cage, next to the driver's corpse. He had enough wits about him to know that the bikers weren't about to ride off into the sunset without taking an insurance shot. Suddenly his worst fears were confirmed. Through the broken front door, he sighted Cherry and his pal coming his way, their guns drawn, their eyes greedy for more blood.

The driver's service revolver was stuck in his gun belt. His body was only inches away from Reggie. Unless Reggie could work himself loose, those inches might as well have been miles. Sweat streamed down his cheeks as he strained to get hold of the gun.

With each new effort, his fingers fell just short of the gun. Grunting with pain, Reggie wormed forward on his stomach and stretched his arm out as far as it would go. He reached for the revolver just as the bikers appeared in the doorway.

Reggie shot first. The bikers hit the pavement and returned the fire. They peppered round after round at the crumpled bus, while Reggie's bullets zinged around their heads. It was two against one, and Reggie was losing.

The bikers almost earned their payoff right then and there. All that stood between Reggie and a trip to eternity was the sudden appearance of two Highway Patrol cars, their blue lights flashing as they raced toward the scene.

"Let's get outta here!" shouted Hickok, making a dash for his bike.

Determined to finish the job, Cherry aimed one more shot before he, too, dashed for his Harley. With the cops already bearing down on them, they released their clutches, popped their choppers into wheelies, and took off down the road.

Next stop, San Francisco.

* * *

The TV had been on all afternoon. It was only when the news began that Price started paying attention.

"Out on U.S. Fifty, the Central Valley area has become the first municipality in the country to claim a bus and a tractor-trailer truck as the victims of a drive-by shooting," announced the television reporter who was doing live on-site coverage of the accident.

Price was hunkered down on the floor of a windowless room in a dockside warehouse in Oakland. On the coffee table in front of him were two bricks of C-4, which he was wiring together into a bomb. Piled neatly next to the bricks were the three bombs he'd constructed during the last several hours while Cherry and Hickok had been creating havoc.

He put down his work and turned up the volume on the TV. The reporter pointed to the chaotic spectacle just behind her. The Department of Corrections bus and the tractor-trailer truck lay on their sides like beached whales. Emergency workers milled about, spraying the vehicles with a chemical foam that lessened the risk of an explosion. In the distance, tractors could be seen retrieving the irrigation pipes and dragging them off the road.

"The collision resulted in two fatalities," continued the reporter. "The bus driver, Dick Reilly of Modesto, and Andrew Scotto, a prisoner being transferred to San Quentin. Both were pronounced dead at the scene. Phil?"

Seated behind his desk at the studio, the local anchorman picked up the thread of the story. "Thank you for that live on-the-scene report, Phyllis," he said, as the image of the accident was transposed onto the screen behind him. "The California Highway Patrol believes that this was an attempted jailbreak gone wrong. They describe the assailants as members of a motorcycle gang, possibly members of the same gang that attacked a roadside diner earlier today."

Price stared at the screen and shook his head in disgust.

"The Highway Patrol expects cleanup to continue throughout the day. In other news"—the anchorman segued into the next item—"attorneys for a coalition of farmers and environmentalists told a state appellate court that it should overturn the approval of a fifty-two-million-dollar coal-burning power plant, citing violations of environmental law that will further damage the area's farming region. Attorneys claim that fifteen thousand pounds of noxious gases and other damaging matter would be discharged daily into the air. When we come back, we'll have the latest weather report."

Price grabbed the remote-control device and clicked off the Power button. After the endless drone of the TV, the room suddenly felt very quiet.

"Get with the program, boys," Price angrily admonished his missing associates.

Then he made himself comfortable again and went back to work, wiring the bombs.

Reggie was pissed off. The bright overhead lighting in the Central Valley Hospital emergency room was hurting his eyes and making his head ache worse than it already did. He'd obliged the doctor by letting him take all the X rays he wanted. He'd even agreed to hang out there on the examination table, while the doctor checked out the X rays and decided whether Reggie was still all in one piece.

However, he was fast losing his patience with the two local representatives of the law who'd barged into the examining room shortly after he'd arrived by ambulance. He'd be wise to cooperate with them, the tall, skinny cop advised him. *Or else,* blustered the stocky, beer-bellied cop.

Reggie was doing his best under the circumstances. But just because he was an ex-con sure as hell didn't mean he had to take responsibility for a fight he hadn't started.

"Hey, man," he told the fat cop for the third time, "I said I was just minding my own business, and then those bikers came along and started shooting at the bus—"

"Your X rays are perfect, Mr. Hammond," the doctor interrupted, sounding as if he himself were personally responsible for Reggie's good fortune.

"Then how come I still have a headache?" demanded Reggie.

"You had a bus roll over on you. Nobody said it wasn't gonna hurt." The tall, thin cop chuckled.

The doctor frowned and continued. "You might have a slight concussion or a subdural hematoma. Either way, you're one lucky man. We'll have to hold you overnight. Then we'll know more in the morning."

"No, I ain't stayin' here overnight," Reggie protested, looking around for his shirt and jacket. "Me and my subdural hematoma are goin' home. I ain't spendin' my first day out in no hospital."

"You're gonna be here until you answer all our questions," the fat cop threatened. "Are you sure you never saw those bikers before?"

"Hey, all you big rednecks look the same to me." Reggie guffawed.

The fat cop suddenly decided he had business elsewhere. "Keep on 'im, Art. I'll be right back," he told his partner.

"Oh, great. I get to spend my first day out of prison with Art the redneck," Reggie grumbled, then came to a decision. No matter what the doctor had to say, he was going to give these boys five more minutes of his valuable time. After that, they were on their own, because he had to be moving on.

Reggie would have been surprised to learn that his old friend Jack Cates was smoking up a storm in a treatment room just across the hall from him. Certainly Cherry Ganz, who'd left Cates for dead, would have been shocked to find Cates alive and well and pacing the floor while he waited to be released.

The emergency-room doctor held up Cates's X rays and said, "You have a hairline fracture of your left clavicle."

"Hmmph," Jack growled. He looked around for an ashtray, found nothing suitable, and flicked the ashes into the palm of his hand.

"Blunt trauma broke the skin," the doctor explained.

"Right." She was young and pretty and he liked her figure. Her blond hair was pulled back behind her ears with a clip. Jack tried to imagine how she would look with it loose around her face. In another lifetime, he might have put the moves on her. But today he was feeling old and tired.

"You're lucky," she said, fanning away the cigarette smoke. "You always wear a bulletproof vest?"

Jack chuckled mirthlessly. "Only when I see my friends."

The doctor reached up, extricated the cigarette from Cates's mouth, and put it out under her heel. She handed Jack a large gauze pad. "I want you to change the bandage on your chest every hour, hour and a half."

"Right." He nodded again. But his mind was on Reggie, not his injuries.

"And we have to immobilize that arm, so wear this sling," the doctor added.

"Thanks, Doc," he said. He took the sling, which he had no intention of using, and shoved his right arm into the sleeve of his sport jacket.

The doctor looked alarmed. "Where are you going? We still have to wait for the lab reports."

Jack grabbed his bullet-ridden vest and headed out into the hallway. He winced as his bad arm made contact with the door.

"I've got police business," he called over his shoulder, lighting up another cigarette.

A highway patrolman stood in the middle of the hall, interviewing the waitress from the diner. "So I was coming out of the kitchen with my arms full of this guy's breakfast," she was saying, still shaking her head from the shock of it all, "and I'm worried because I don't want to be late. He's got this funny look on his face. Not just like he's hungry, 'cause I see that all the time, but like he's mad about something." She took a deep breath, made sure the policeman was writing down every word, and continued. "Then there's these big sounds like guns going off, and the front window breaks, and I hear someone screaming, and I guess it's me. But then I see he's shot, and I drop the plates and they break and"—she wrung her hands, reliving her guilt—"I wanna go help him, and I don't know what to do . . . I don't help him."

The waitress prided herself on being tough. Now, however, she couldn't hold back her tears at the memory of her customer's writhing in pain on the floor. It must have been a miracle that had kept him alive until the ambulance showed up. Earlier, a doctor had told her not to worry, that the man's wounds weren't serious. But she'd seen all those bullets flying into him . . . all that blood . . .

The policeman waited patiently while the waitress dabbed at her cheeks with a tissue. And suddenly, there was her customer, charging down the hall like a bull in heat. Her eyes widened with shock. How on earth . . . ? Who was this guy, anyway? Superman?

She grabbed at his sleeve as he rushed past, but Cates didn't even throw a nod in her direction.

"Reggie Hammond," he barked at the cop who'd been questioning Reggie a few minutes earlier. "So when can I get him?"

The cop shrugged. "If it was up to me, I'd help you, but they gotta keep him overnight. You know, observation. This is one lucky guy. I'd like to follow him around at the racetrack, know what I mean?"

Cates figured that if Reggie needed observing, he was the one to do it. Lucky? Ha! That was a laugh. Reggie Hammond's luck was about to run out—unless he started being *very* cooperative *very* fast.

He gestured to the cop to step aside, looked around to make sure this was just between the two of them, and said quietly, "You know what that guy was in the joint for?"

The cop shook his head no.

"That son-of-a-bitch." Cates looked pained as he dropped his bomb. "He's a child-molester. He's involved in kiddy porn. Now I've got to get him back to San Francisco by tonight to identify the kingpin of the organization. Otherwise, the kingpin walks. Listen," he said, leaning closer to the cop, "you got any kids?"

"Yeah," the cop said, wishing now that Hammond had taken more of a beating from the bikers. "Two little girls. Take him."

Reggie was fixing his tie in front of the mirror above the sink when Cates showed up in his room.

"Hey, Reggie," he offered, "wanna go for a ride in a Cadillac?"

Some days it almost didn't pay to get out of jail, Reggie thought. Why wasn't he surprised to see Cates's big, ugly puss grinning at him like a Halloween jack-o'-lantern? No wonder those two cops had suddenly done such a fast disappearing act. Reggie wondered what kind of rank Cates had pulled on them in order for them to be willing to give him up so quickly.

Well, maybe Cates could impress these redneck country boys, but Reggie Hammond was too much of a city dude ever again to fall for his jive.

"Leave me the fuck alone. I'm having a bad day, and you're not making it any better," he said with a snarl to Cates.

Cates held up his hands, a gesture of appeasement. "Come on, Reg. I'm just tryin' to help you out," he said smoothly. "Of course, you could always catch another bus. You had plenty of luck on the last one. . . ."

Reggie brushed back his hair and straightened his tie.

"I've got nothin' to say to you, Jack," he snapped. "Good-bye."

"Sorry, Reggie." Cates positioned himself so that his burly shoulders blocked the doorway.

The two men stared at each other. Reggie was younger and in better shape, but Jack was taller and heftier. There was little or no chance of Reggie's getting past the cop without his permission, and they both knew it.

Cates laid it on the line. "They've released you in my custody. You're screwed."

Reggie didn't flinch. What the hell? After all, he did need a lift back to San Francisco. Cates was a terror on the road, but it sure beat another bus ride to nowhere. Besides which, there was still the matter of Reggie's half-million to be resolved. He brushed the dirt off his jacket, then pulled at his cuffs and strode out of the emergency room, with Cates close behind him.

"Okay, let's get down to business," Jack said gruffly, more pleased to have Reggie's company than he ever would have admitted. "You ever seen those bikers before?"

"My memory improves when I got money in my pocket," Reggie coldly informed him, as they walked down the hospital corridor.

"You know the rules, Reggie," Jack growled. "As soon as you tell me why the Iceman wants you dead, I'll think about giving you the money."

There was just one little detail that Cates seemed to have forgotten. Last time around, Reggie had been a con on a forty-eight-hour furlough. He didn't have much choice about playing by Cates's rules. As of today, however, the rules had changed. The sooner

Cates figured that out, the better off they'd both be. If the cop wanted Reggie's help, he would have to pay for it in advance.

"Why don't you ask the guy you got my picture from?" Reggie demanded.

"He's not talking real good anymore. I killed him," Cates said gruffly.

Reggie smirked as Cates got the front door for him. "Way to go, Jack. Smooth. They pay you by the pound, or what?"

Cates puffed furiously on his cigarette and followed Reggie down the hospital steps. "He shot at me first. Only . . . we can't find his gun. That's why I'm in the shit house."

Reggie couldn't believe what he was hearing. "You're askin' me for sympathy? You're askin' the wrong guy! I was supposed to be on my way to catch a plane to Miami Beach to run a little used-car lot with my uncle. Porsches. Classics," he angrily informed Cates. "Instead, I'm broke, shot at, glass all over my suit and hair and shit, had a bus go flying in the air, roll over, break my Walkman, get hit by a big-ass truck."

"Hey, I ran into your friends today, too. Took six slugs in the chest," Cates protested.

"Yeah? You're doing pretty good for a dead man."

"Would be, if it wasn't for this," Cates said, dangling his vest in front of Reggie's face.

Reggie inspected the damage and gave a long, low whistle. Someone sure was eager to see Cates dead. "How come you was wearin' one of these?" he asked as he handled the flak vest.

"I knew people were tryin' to kill you." Jack

chuckled. "Shit, I'd hate to be killed by some stray bullet that had your name on it. That'd be a lousy way to go, wouldn't it?"

"You're all heart," Reggie said dryly, handing back the vest. "I might need me one of these."

"Sure. They got 'em all over. Department stores, sporting-goods stores. They run about seven hundred and fifty bucks. A little more than they gave you when they let you out, right?"

Reggie was too pissed off to reply to the cop's joke at his expense. He kept his mouth shut until he was halfway across the parking lot, when he spotted Jack's Cadillac. Ungainly though it was, the Caddy reminded him of the sweet little Porsche he'd left in Cates's care. Many a night in prison, he'd dreamed of that Porsche . . . and of all the women who'd leaned up close to him in the front seat.

"You still got my car, Jack?" he asked, half afraid to hear the answer. *Because if you don't, you're going to need more than a vest to protect you.*

"No problem, Reggie. All safe and sound back in the city," Jack assured him. "I took real good care of it for you. Just like I said I would."

Cates had also said he'd visit Reggie in prison—and never bothered to show up. He'd promised to return Reggie's money. Now he was threatening to hold on to it unless Reggie teamed up with him again. True, they worked well together. But a man needed a partner he could count on. Cates had betrayed him, and Reggie couldn't see any reason why he should put his trust in Cates again.

"Jack, look, I can't believe this," he said, suddenly remembering the taste of the bitterness he'd swallowed day after day for five long years. "You and me had something together. Now you're acting like an asshole and stealin' my money. You're fuckin' me, Jack."

Cates glared at Reggie. "I'm fuckin' you?" The guy had it all backward, Cates thought. "You fucked yourself. I checked into it. There was a payroll robbery out at the prison. They found the money in your cell."

"I got set up," Reggie said flatly, opening the car door.

"Yeah, you got framed," said Cates, walking around to the driver's side.

Five years ago, after they'd spent two days together chasing down a couple of real bad characters, Jack Cates would have sworn that Reggie Hammond was a stand-up guy. He'd flat-out admitted to his boss that Reggie was smarter and gutsier than any other guy he'd ever partnered.

Then Reggie had gone and proved him wrong. Betrayed Jack's trust in him. Now Cates was asking for Reggie's help because he had no other choice. Sure, he got framed. "That's what every crook says," he reminded Reggie.

"They couldn't find your bad guy's gun, could they, Jack?"

Cates threw Reggie a dirty look as he fished for his keys. "That's different."

"How?" asked Reggie, stretching his legs out in front of him. The Caddy was an ugly monster of a car, and normally he wouldn't have been caught dead in it. But it had its advantages—first and foremost, it had plenty of room to spread out.

"I'm a cop," Jack stated the obvious. "You're a crook."

"I knew you were going to say that." Reggie spat on

his pinky ring and polished it on the sleeve of his jacket. His eyes flashed with anger as he folded his arms across his chest. "I'm a crook, so just screw Reggie Hammond, right?"

"Right." Jack nodded. The answer came easily enough. In his heart he wasn't sure it was that simple. The fact was, he could name plenty of people he wanted to make trouble for—but Reggie Hammond wasn't one of them. Anyway, from the look of things, Reggie did such a good job of screwing himself that he didn't have to worry about getting screwed by Cates or anyone else.

The payroll robbery . . . To this day, Jack couldn't come up with a reason why Reggie had tried to pull off such a dumb stunt. The guy could be a real asshole, no doubt about it, but he was a *smart* asshole. Not to mention that he'd already stashed away a big fat pile of cash, so it wasn't as if he needed the money.

Jack was disappointed when he'd heard about the attempted heist. It had forced him to face a fact of life—a crook was a crook. Even Reggie Hammond. Especially Reggie Hammond.

So, yeah, okay . . . screw him! He could go to hell, for all Jack cared, but first he had some talking to do.

What Reggie had to say now, however, wasn't what Cates wanted to hear. "I'm cold on you, Cates. You and me are right back where we started from before we ever met," he announced. "Just take me to my car, man."

Jack flinched as he turned over the ignition.

"You hurt?" Reggie asked.

"Yeah." Jack grunted. "My shoulder. Thanks to your friends."

"It hurt real bad?" Reggie sounded sympathetic.

"Yeah," said Cates, wishing he'd thought to ask the doctor for a couple of pain-killers.

Reggie settled back against his seat and closed his eyes. "Good," he said with a smile, and then he fell asleep.

7

An hour out of San Francisco, Reggie awoke with a raging headache, feeling confused and disoriented. Where the hell was he? he wondered. This car . . . the open highway . . . Cates hunched over the wheel, glowering at the setting sun. Suddenly it all came back to him. He was going home—wherever that might be.

Recently, in a rare philosophical moment, Reggie had realized that playing the field with the ladies had its disadvantages. There was no special honey who'd kept the home fires burning for him. Nor was there anyone who was getting herself all prettied up tonight waiting for him to ring her bell.

As for family, the closest thing he had to a relative was his uncle down in Miami. And what Reggie had told Cates about them running the Porsche dealership together wasn't exactly the whole story. The truth was, his uncle had been less than thrilled to hear from him after all these years. He'd halfheartedly agreed to give Reggie a job—"as long as you can stay out of trouble," he'd written, heavily underscoring his warning.

So now here was Reggie, without a clue as to where he would be staying this evening, which was kind of a strange idea for a man who'd spent the last few years behind bars. Not that he was worried. He'd make out fine, just the same as always, once he settled up with Cates.

"Say," said Reggie, startling Jack out of his reverie, "how much of my money did you spend, anyway?"

"About twenty-five grand. You said I could buy a new car," Cates reminded him.

Reggie regretted his misplaced generosity. "Where is it?" he asked.

Jack threw him a dirty look. What a wiseguy. "This *is* the new car."

"This?" Reggie rolled his eyes. Some people never learned. "Looks like the same old piece of shit sky-blue Cadillac you had before."

"Bought the same model, year, and color. Everything's the same," said Jack. "I get attached to things."

"Speaking of which, how's that lady of yours?"

"Elaine? She married me. Five years ago. Drove me over to city hall for a quick ceremony. Figured to settle me down. We even bought a damned house."

Reggie chuckled. "You must look real good out there, cuttin' the grass."

"Yeah," Jack growled, the tip of his cigarette glowing in the dusk that was falling around them. "Dinner every night. Clean clothes . . ." An image of Elaine, her wavy red hair flowing down her back, flashed before him.

"Sounds like where I been."

Jack caught the note of bitterness and told him, "Felt like it. She left me after a year and a half. Ah, I really don't want to talk about it. . . ." His voice trailed off into the darkness.

That's when he'd really begun to drink heavily—not just Scotch, but beer and vodka and anything else that could numb the pain. He'd never believed he was meant to be a husband, but he'd loved Elaine enough to marry her. He'd hated himself a lot for a long time after she walked out on him.

"That's it, Jack, hide the hurt," Reggie said sarcastically, never expecting what followed.

It was as if a trapdoor to Cates's emotions had suddenly sprung open, releasing a torrent of memories and grievances that he'd squirreled away.

"First coupla weeks were pretty good. Then her mother moved in with us," he grouched. "Elaine started buyin' these dresses. She wanted credit cards—American Express, Visa, MasterCard . . ." He shook his head, remembering how they'd fought over those credit cards. And everything else. "First month she bought two French poodles that shit all over the place. She always wanted sex. . . . I'd come home from a stakeout, twenty-four hours without sleep, and she's waitin' in lingerie."

Sounds pretty good to me, Reggie thought, and he was about to say so. But now that Cates had gotten started on his trip down memory lane, there was no stopping him.

"I got her this house at the police auction. It used to be a crack house," he went on. "Then she says it's not big enough, not in a good enough neighborhood. Says I don't give her gifts, just evidence. Got her a great diamond ring. Then the trial came up and she didn't wanna give it back."

They'd had a hell of an argument over that one. How the hell was he supposed to know the bastards would go to trial instead of copping a plea?

"The house was full of honeydew: 'Honey, do this. Honey, do that.' Then it got bad. She called me a male chauvinist pig. A slob. Said I smelled, watched too much sports on TV. Said I wasn't sensitive to her needs. Said I was hostile and uncommunicative. Hell with it," said Cates, summing it all up for Reggie, in case he'd missed the point. "She was a real nice girl, but maybe I wasn't cut out for bein' hooked up on a permanent basis."

For once, Reggie was speechless. Since when had he signed up to be Cates's psychiatrist? The guy should never have gotten married. Reggie could have told him that in a second. Too bad Cates had never bothered to come around to visit and ask his advice.

Massaging his aching forehead, he punctuated Cates's story with a loud yawn. "Right," he said, and promptly fell back to sleep.

The next time Reggie woke up, they'd turned off the highway and were driving down a street in Sunset, close to the beach, not far from the zoo. Cates saw that he was awake and gestured to a small house with a big FOR SALE sign out front. Making a wide U-turn, he swung around and pulled up at the curb.

Even by the dim light of the streetlights, Reggie could see that Cates wasn't a model homeowner. The lawn was overgrown, the bushes unkempt, and the paint on the house, peeling. The property needed work.

"This is where we lived till we split up and she moved to Mill Valley. I been trying to sell it," Jack said, explaining the obvious. "Twelve grand of your money paid for the down payment."

Reggie turned toward Cates and frowned, feeling his anger rising to the surface. But he kept his mouth shut until he looked back at the house and saw his beautiful Porsche Speedster parked in Cates's driveway. Then he lost his cool.

"How could you leave my car outside like that? Look at the dirt all over it. What if somebody would have stole it? Why didn't you put it in the garage?"

"Nobody's gonna steal your fucking car." Jack interrupted Reggie's tirade. "I had an alarm put in. Here." He handed Reggie the keyring alarm. "Now just push that blue button—"

Reggie grabbed the keyring and opened the car door, slamming it behind him. As he turned toward his Porsche, Jack got out of the Caddy and walked around the front of the car to join him.

"You have no appreciation whatsoever for what's hype." Reggie continued his verbal assault on Cates. "That's what it is. You don't know that car flies. You know how much pussy I got because of that car?" Reggie's question hung in the air as he held the alarm and glared at Cates while pointing the alarm out in front of him. Following Cates's instructions, he pressed the keyring alarm button.

The first thing they heard was an unfamiliar beeping sound. Right after that came an ear-splitting boom that sent shock waves through the night air. Jack and Reggie, standing on the lawn a few feet away from the car, threw themselves to the ground. They watched in stunned silence as the Porsche burst into flames. Splinters of blazing steel splattered across the yard, like tiny Roman candles.

Cates had his gun cocked and ready. But all that emerged from the bushes was a pair of chipmunks whose sleep had been disturbed by the explosion.

Reggie stood up and stared openmouthed at the bonfire that was once his beloved car, wondering how he'd landed in the middle of this nightmare. "They blew up my car," he muttered. They blew up my car!"

"It's a damn shame," Jack muttered, almost meaning it.

"They blew up my fuckin car and all you've got to say is it's a damn shame?"

In case Reggie needed to be reminded, Cates went down the list for him. "No car. No money. You're havin' a bad day."

Reggie couldn't take any more shit from Cates. "That's it man. I'm calling some of my homies. I'm gettin' a fuckin' loan and I'm steppin' off. You are bad news, bad luck—and I'm finished with you." Hoping that Cates had finally gotten the message, Reggie turned and stalked away.

The police cars turned up first, followed moments later by a couple of screeching fire trucks. Jack and Reggie gave their statements to the cops, then took off for police headquarters downtown. Jack was in a hurry to figure out the connection between the barbecued Porsche and the biker who'd used him for target practice that morning. While Reggie cooled his heels in the Caddy, which was parked in a no-standing zone, Jack headed for the detectives' squad room.

He stopped first at the message desk and flipped through the latest printouts and bulletins.

"Jack!" called Kehoe, hurrying to catch up with him.

"Yeah?"

"What the hell is going on?" demanded Kehoe. "We got a report you're shot, your house blew up—"

"No," Jack brusquely interrupted him. "Wasn't my house, it was a car."

"Fire department's still out there," Kehoe went on. "Your car blew up?"

"No," Jack said impatiently. "It wasn't my car. It was some other guy's car parked in front of my house. Listen, did anything come in on those descriptions of the bikers that hit the prison bus?"

Sensing that he couldn't get any more information out of Cates, Kehoe shook his head. "Not yet, I'll check again. Look, Jack, do me a favor. Go see Wilson. He told me if you don't go see him, he's gonna send someone out to bring you in."

"Oh, shit!" Jack sighed, tossing the file folder he'd been examining.

As he walked down the hall, he passed Cruise, who took one look at him and said, "Hey, Jack, you okay?"

His mind elsewhere, Jack brushed past him and made his way over to Wilson's cubicle. He tapped on the door, then opened it without waiting for a response.

Wilson was seated at his desk, his head buried in his files. Looking up, he said, "Hello, Jack."

Jack closed the door behind him and waited for Wilson's attack.

It wasn't long in coming. "Boy, oh, boy," the inspector declared, rising from his chair and beginning to pace the room. "First, the motorcycle track. Then the diner. Now we got a bomb at your house. I suppose the Iceman is responsible for all of it?"

"Yeah," Jack agreed, well aware that Wilson was toying with him. "That's what I figure."

"Well, I'm not going to stand here and argue with you. Man to man, I'm here to support you," Wilson informed him. "However, as supervisor of Internal Affairs, I do have to remind you that you are still on suspension, at least until the court hearing tomorrow. I'm gonna need your gun, your badge, and your police I.D."

"Right," Jack conceded, knowing he had no alternative but to hand them over.

"I'll bet you think I enjoy this, don't you?" Wilson asked, his tone softening. "Jack, do me a favor. Go home and get some sleep."

Jack nodded. "I just gotta check on a few things. Make out some reports," he said, hoping Wilson would buy his line. He turned to go, then changed his mind. He couldn't leave without letting Wilson know what he really thought. "You know, I don't mind people checking up on cops. I don't think we're above the law. But making cops do it . . . it's bad for morale, bad for cops. Let civilians do it. You're a real chickenshit, Wilson. Maybe it's not your fault. Maybe it's your job."

He held Wilson's glance for a moment. Then he was out the door before Wilson had a chance to open his mouth.

* * *

While Jack was turning over his badge and gun, Reggie was feeding a pay phone with the change he'd gotten for one of the twenties the warden had handed him. He'd already gotten to the T's in his little black book, and nobody seemed to be home for him.

Things certainly had changed in the last five years. Just about everyone had answering machines, and if you didn't feel like waiting for the sound of the beep, tough luck to you, brother. Either that, or a lot of people weren't in the mood to talk tonight, because Reggie was on the receiving end of some very chilly hangups.

Keeping his eye on the street, Reggie dialed yet another number and checked his watch as two patrolmen, just going on duty, walked through the arched entranceway of the police building and headed for Cates's Caddy, which was parked in a red zone.

"Hey, Marvin!" Reggie warmly greeted one of his buddies from the good old days. "Reggie Hammond . . . Hammond. H-A-M— Right! No, I ain't dead. Look, I'm out and I need— What? Outta prison. Yeah."

"What? You gone straight?" *The guy must be kidding!*

"Jesus? You? I don't believe— No, I think that's great, it's just— Hello? Hello?" he shouted into the dead receiver. "Born-again asshole!"

He crossed out Marvin Thomas's name and deposited another twenty-five cents in the coin slots. He was quickly running as short on change as he was on folks to call.

As he waited for his next call to connect, Reggie looked over at the younger of the two cops.

"Somebody's got some balls parking illegally right in front of the precinct," the cop announced loudly enough for Reggie to hear.

Reggie stuck his head out of the booth. "He hates cops," he said conversationally.

"He does, huh?" The cop frowned.

"Yeah. He gave me a lift downtown. He thinks cops are all pussies who hide behind their badges. I told him not to park here. He wouldn't listen. He's got this blatant disregard for the law." Reggie's voice oozed with the respect *he* felt for the law.

The phone was ringing at the other end as the cop began writing Cates a parking ticket.

"Leroy?" Reggie said hopefully. "Oh, Mrs. Womack. Uh . . . this is Reggie Hammond. Could I talk to Leroy? . . . No, I'm not dead. . . . I don't care what you heard. Look, is Leroy home? Put the man on the telephone."

While he waited for Leroy and wondered who was spreading the premature rumors of his death, he turned back to the cop and asked, "What's that, like a hundred-dollar fine?"

The cop slapped his book shut. "Nah, forty bucks."

"That's it? I'd check the registration, then, while you're at it. I'll bet it's expired," Reggie said helpfully.

The cop walked around to the back of the car and checked the rear license plate. "Yeah, it is." He nodded. "Thanks."

Reggie smiled broadly as the cop reopened his book and wrote out a second citation. "Don't mention it," he said.

He was feeling a lot more cheerful by the time his friend came on the line.

"Leroy? That you, man? . . . All right!" He crowed.

"It's Reggie Hammond. I'm out. . . . No, I'm in town. . . . Yes, I know, but I can't get out yet. That's why I called. I need some bread. . . . No, a loan. . . . What? What are you talkin' about, collateral?" He couldn't believe this shit he was hearing. "It's me, Reggie. . . . Hello?"

Leroy had hung up on him.

"Dick," he said, banging down the phone.

He flipped through the rest of his phone book, but every page was filled with crossed-out names of people who thought Reggie was dead or yesterday's news. Apparently someone was spreading the word that he was persona non grata. Reggie had a pretty good idea who that someone might be.

He tossed his phone book into the garbage, resettled himself in the Caddy, and had the satisfaction of watching the cop stick the tickets under Cates's windshield wiper.

"Your friend's not too smart," he told Reggie.

"Tell me about it. Takes him an hour and a half to watch 'Sixty Minutes.'" Reggie chuckled smugly. "He's a big, dumb cop named Jack Cates."

"Shit!" The cop slammed his book against the car. He'd messed up. He should have recognized Cates's big blue monster. The tickets were already written, so he couldn't tear them up. But there was no way Cates would pay them. And, by the way, the cop thought, who was this black guy who'd made himself at home in Cates's front seat?

Glowering at Reggie, he said, "Tell that big asshole to stop parking in front of the station. He's not gonna be able to get away with it in a couple of days."

"I'll tell him," Reggie solemnly agreed. "You can count on that."

8

For months after the computer system had first been installed, Jack stubbornly resisted getting acquainted with its charms. While his colleagues dutifully learned how to plug into the nationwide network of information, Jack excused himself from class and went his own way. While they happily tapped at the keyboard, calling up words and pictures on their screens, Jack would glare at the machine on his desk, daring it to tell him something he didn't already know.

In the end, he'd had to spend a lot of late nights teaching himself the program, because, to his chagrin, he eventually discovered that the computer, teamed with the printer, could work wonders. It could send him portraits of suspects who were wanted in cities across the country, and match their prints with the ones he had in his hand. It could spit out lists of criminal complaints and M.O.'s that proved to be invaluable in tracing someone who'd fled the scene or jumped bail.

The computer could even generate mug shots based on an eyewitness's description. Press the right key, and a drawing would begin to emerge on the screen that could ultimately add up to an astonishingly close likeness of an alleged perpetrator.

Tonight Jack was pressing a lot of right keys. The laser printer had already spit out a computer-generated mug shot of the biker who'd ambushed him in the diner. Now Jack was working on a composite of the black man with the briefcase who'd been the last person to speak to the dead mechanic.

The menu line across the top of the screen identified the program: National Crime Information Computer, Physical Description Form. Underneath it, one-half of the computer screen displayed a crude picture of a man's face. The other half offered a list of facial characteristics that ran the gamut from nose, eyes, and mouth to identifiable scars or other distinguishing marks.

Jack's reading glasses were smudged with cigarette ashes, but he was concentrating too heavily to notice as he chose among the variations that the program had to offer.

Narrower? asked the computer, highlighting the nose on the screen. Jack punched the "Y" key to signal "Yes."

Wider forehead? asked the computer. Again Jack punched the "Y" for "Yes."

He went down the list, matching the descriptive options to facial features. The drawing on the screen changed with each selection. The finished product was a remarkably faithful rendering of the black man's face.

Jack pressed the Print button and lit a cigarette. While he waited for the hard copy, he began checking the pictures in the mug book. He hadn't gotten very far when Kehoe dropped a sheet of printout paper on his desk.

"Here you go, Jack," Kehoe said. "Three complaints involving biker types in the last four days. Two traffics and a D and D."

Jack glanced at the sheet and stuffed it in his pocket, then tore the finished copies off the printer. He held up the copies of the computer-created mug shots—the biker and the black man from the track. "Thanks. Run these guys through N.C.I.C?" he asked.

"All right. I'll have Cruise run 'em." Kehoe nodded and glanced at the shot of the black man. "Don't look much like a biker to me. Is it?"

Jack was already on his way out the door and didn't hear Kehoe's last question. Too many questions of his own were whirling around in his mind.

The first one he asked of Reggie, when he found him standing outside, next to his Caddy. "You still here?" he growled. "I didn't think you were gonna stick around."

"You think I want to? Guess again," Reggie told him. "I was supposed to be a free man, money in my pocket, and getting on with my life. Last thing I wanted was to be tied to your big, dumb white ass again."

Cates shrugged. Whoever said life was fair? "Welcome back, Reggie."

Reggie had spent the last hour doing some hard

thinking about his situation, and Jack's. Fate had thrown them together again, for better or for worse, just as it was said in marriage vows. And, as in any good marriage, if they were going to be partners, even temporarily, they would both have to make some compromises—because they both had everything to lose if they didn't.

Reggie had composed a short speech setting forth his terms, which he expected Jack to meet if he wanted his help. "Let me tell you one thing, Jack," Reggie said now, shaking a finger at Cates. "I'm not a convict on a weekend pass this time. I'm a free man. And you, you're an inch away from where I was yesterday—living in a cell. So you're not running things. I'm not working for you. I don't trust you. I don't even like you. Got it?"

Bored by Reggie's lecture, Cates yawned conspicuously and demanded, "Just give me something I can use."

"How's this?" Reggie delivered the punch line to the joke he'd been enjoying since Cates had admitted to being a homeowner. "The Iceman bought your house."

Jack gaped at him. "What the hell are you talking about?"

"You didn't figure it out?" said Reggie, gratified by Cates's reaction. "The Iceman's the drug dealer Ganz and me and my gang robbed of that half a million dollars you were supposed to keep safe for me, and he's still pissed off. It's disgusting how important people think money is, right, Jack?"

"Holy shit!" Jack exclaimed, blown away by what Reggie was telling him.

If any other con had tried to feed him that line, he

never would have bought the story, it was so far-fetched. But what Reggie was saying smacked of the truth. It also went a long way toward explaining the bizarre series of coincidences that had started with his finding Reggie's picture in the dead mechanic's gym bag.

Reggie slapped his knee and cackled with pleasure. "Yeah. Four years you can't get your hands on the Iceman, and he paid for the down payment on your house and your piece-of-shit Cadillac. Is that good enough?"

"Pretty good," Cates conceded, still digesting the information.

"It gets better," Reggie promised. "Get in the car."

Jack was about to tell him to shove it, because *he* gave the orders around here. Then he decided that this one time he'd make an exception and let Reggie have his cheap thrill.

But Reggie wasn't through issuing orders. "No," he said, as Cates headed for the driver's side of the car. "You get on the other side. I'm driving. You got one arm, and I don't want another wreck. I'm not like you. I got a lot to live for."

Before Cates could even open his mouth, Reggie had opened the driver's door and slid behind the wheel. Jack shrugged and walked around to the other side of the Caddy. "I always wanted a chauffeur, Reggie," he said with a smirk.

But Reggie had the last laugh as he jammed on the gas pedal and peeled off down the street. He'd waited five years to show Cates how *he* handled a car. And from the look on Jack's face, he wasn't too thrilled to leave the driving to Reggie.

"One of those crazy-ass bikers that hit the bus

today? I recognized him," Reggie admitted, slowing at a Stop sign. "Albert Ganz's brother, Cherry. He's a psycho. Makes his brother look like Gandhi."

"Ganz's *brother?"* Cates's mouth dropped open. How many more bombs was Reggie planning to drop on him today?

"You heard me."

Jack needed some help with this one. "Why would the Iceman hire the brother of one of the guys who robbed him to kill us?" he asked.

"I ratted his brother to you the last time we spent forty-eight hours together and you shot his ass off till he stopped breathing. Do you know anybody who'd want to kill us more?" demanded Reggie, wondering whether Cates was getting so old that his brain had gone soft.

"Good point." Cates acknowledged the logic of the Iceman's reasoning.

"Ganz said Cherry had this bitch, Angel," Reggie went on. "All he talked about was what a great piece of ass she was. Danced at a bar downtown called Barnstormers—if you call that dancing."

"I got a complaint here that a couple of bikers rousted a bar called Barnstormers," Cates told him, sure that they were finally getting somewhere.

Reggie raised a skeptical eyebrow. "You mean the police are makin' a contribution to this investigation? I'm amazed."

Cates had a better question for him. "Wait a minute," he said suspiciously. "You were in a gang with this guy's brother and you remember where his girlfriend works after five years on the rock?"

"That's right," Reggie shot back. "Stories about

pussy are the only thing worth remembering in prison."

Jack couldn't argue with that. Nor was he much in the mood for conversation. His arm was killing him, and his pride was still hurting from having had to surrender his gun and badge. Reggie seemed to know his way to Barnstormers. So Cates settled back and kept his mouth shut until the Caddy rumbled to a stop in front of the bar.

Jack was about to get out of the car when he realized he'd forgotten something. Opening the glove compartment, he pulled out a shiny silver badge that Elaine had once bought him as a joke.

Reggie took one look at the plastic badge in Cates's hand and said, "What you got there?"

"Badge. Helps to have one. Especially when you question someone," Jack said, trying not to sound defensive.

"Jack, that isn't real," Reggie pointed out helpfully, just in case Cates hadn't figured that out.

"So what?" Cates grunted. "Most people can't tell the difference when you flash it."

The guy was definitely going soft in the brain. "It's a toy," Reggie said disgustedly. "Cops-'n'-robbers shit."

Jack knew what he was doing, and his answer to Reggie was short and sweet. "Tough titty," he said, stuffing the badge in his breast pocket and heading into the bar.

Inside the place was jumping. Wall-to-wall couples danced wildly to the pulsing rhythms of a rock band, whose lead singer strutted back and forth across the stage. Two cowboy-hatted women, dressed mostly in sequins and spangles, shimmied their way up and down a runway, as a rooting section of unattached men roared their approval.

Jack and Reggie elbowed a path through the room, which reeked of cigarette smoke and stale beer. Reggie found himself a place at the bar, where he could take in the floor show, while Cates moved right in on the bartender.

Flashing his fake badge at the woman, he shouted above the din, "You the one who called in with a complaint about some bikers?"

For the first time that day, luck was on his side.

"Call the six o'clock news," snapped Terry, barely glancing at his badge. "The cops finally responded to a call. It's only been a day and a half, ya know."

"Sorry," Cates said curtly. "A lot of problems out there in the city."

Terry was unimpressed. She was a taxpayer—most of the time—and she didn't see why her problems had to take a backseat to anyone else's.

Pouring a couple of double whiskeys, she said, "I'll remember that next time I get to vote whether or not you guys get a pay raise."

"You want to tell me what happened, or do you want to bitch a little more?" demanded Cates.

"I want to bitch a little more," said Terry, changing her mind in the next breath and telling her story. "Three motorcycle guys come in here yesterday afternoon. Ordered drinks. Then one of them whispers in my ear . . . tells me he wants me to suck his cock. How's that for sexual harassment?"

"Pretty good. I'd say a six on a scale of ten."

Terry gave him a dirty look and went on. "The guy with the dark hair asks about this girl who used to work in here. Then he gets rough and starts tryin' to grab my boob. Cute, huh? Then the blond one pulls a gun. Slams it down right on the counter. Maybe that's a nine out of ten?"

"What about the girl?"

"Angel Allen? She stopped workin' here about a year ago. Anyway, she dances at some joint in the Tenderloin now. Lives down there. Hey, aren't you supposed to be writing this down?"

"I got a photographic memory," Cates assured her. "You know where she lives?"

"King Mei Hotel. . . . You sure you're a cop?" Terry asked dubiously, wondering if she should ask to see his badge again.

Cates leaned closer and blew smoke in her face. "Keep going. I want to get your story straight."

Reggie, meanwhile, positioned himself as far from Cates as he could manage. Having watched the guy at work before, he didn't want to be in the line of fire when the sparks started flying. The guy had no subtlety, no finesse.

"Vodka," he ordered from the bartender at his end of the bar.

Sipping his drink slowly, he feasted his eyes on the well-endowed dancers who were twirling their tassels to the beat of the bass guitar. A feeling of pressure against his leg made him look up to discover that he was rubbing thighs with a voluptuous black woman who'd squeezed in between him and the customer sitting on the next stool.

"Hello. Hey, nice to meet you," he said, taking in her low-cut, very revealing mini dress. Obviously the chick was interested in him—and who could blame her? How often did such a cool, good-looking brother show up at a place like this? It wouldn't take much to make this lady. He could already hear her groaning under his touch.

"Hi," she purred. "Buy me a drink?"

"Sorry, baby," said Reggie, flashing his most charming smile. Confident of success, he went for the truth and admitted, "I'm almost broke. How about buying me one?"

The light in her eyes instantly vanished. The smile disappeared just as quickly.

"Fuck off," she said succinctly, and was gone faster than Reggie could blink.

"Honesty. I like that in a chick," he announced to no one in particular.

He took another sip of his drink and noticed that the girl had relocated herself several stools down the bar and was coming on to another customer. The man, who was dressed like Reggie in an expensive, well-tailored suit, was obviously falling for her line. Sure, he nodded, raising a hand to summon the bartender. He'd love to buy her a drink.

The mark never felt the girl slip her hand inside his pocket and deftly relieve him of his wallet. A moment later, when he turned to hand her a drink, she smiled sweetly and pointed to the ladies' room.

Reggie chuckled as he watched the show. He'd been away too long, if he'd almost fallen for that old routine. She was a real pro, no doubt about it, and he couldn't help but admire her artistry.

Drink in hand, Reggie worked his way over to the pickpocket victim, who was looking dreamy-eyed with anticipation. "How's it going?" he said.

The man gave a tight little smile. Clearly he had other things on his mind.

"You ever see those traveler's-checks ads, where Karl Malden shows you those stupid tourists, gettin' their pockets picked in slow motion?" asked Reggie.

The man glanced blankly at him, then suddenly figured out what Reggie was getting at. He stuck his hand in his pocket and came up empty. "Shit!" he swore.

"Relax, relax. Don't get your balls all in an uproar. I can get your wallet back," Reggie said calmly.

"How much?" asked the man, who knew there had to be a price tag attached to this offer.

"Half of what you got."

"But—"

Reggie backed away and raised his hands, as if to say, That's my offer, take it or leave it. "Oh, you like having no money, is that it?" he said, taunting the mark. "Okay. But it's a drag canceling credit cards, callin' all those people. . . . All that time some guy's out there runnin' up huge bills in your name, credit rating goes to shit . . . takes months to get it all straightened out."

Reggie saw the struggle in the man's eyes and then turned to leave.

That clinched it. "It's a deal," the man said sullenly, then settled down at the bar to wait for his wallet.

Two women were just leaving the ladies' room as Reggie walked in. They barely gave him a second glance. Barnstormers was that kind of a place. But the pickpocket, who was primping in front of the mirror, took one look at his face and knew he was bad news.

"I just wanted to get to know you a little better," Reggie said sociably, joining her at the mirror. "That was a slick job you did out there. I seen a few, but that was real smooth." He patted down his hair. "I promised that guy out there I'd get him his money back. Now, if you'd like to offer me a little bribe . . . I can tell him you were too fast for me. . . ."

"I *am* too fast for you, sucker!" she hissed, flicking a switchblade at him.

Reggie threw up his arms and backed off. "In my day, a pickpocket didn't need violence," he said.

The woman swung the blade at him and snapped, "Times change."

Maybe so, but Reggie was still smarter, faster, and slicker than the average thief. Before she knew what was happening, he pounced at her, wresting the knife out of her hand. The woman screamed and took a wild swing at him, but Reggie was way ahead of her. He grabbed her arm and pinned it against her back as he spun her around. "I knew we'd be good friends," he murmured into her ear. "Now, where's the money?"

"Find it, tough guy!" she spat.

"Okay," Reggie said enthusiastically. It would be his pleasure. He didn't need a road map to figure out where she'd hidden it. Reaching down the front of her top, he let his fingers linger on her breasts as he felt for the bills.

Just then the bathroom door swung open. A girl gawked at him.

Reggie faked a smile. "Almost done," he said, his hand halfway down the pickpocket's dress.

The customer turned and left the room without a word.

Reggie resumed his hunt for buried treasure. "Aha!" he announced as his hand closed around the cash. Triumphantly waving the money under her nose, he leered at the woman and said, "I been in prison a lot of years. You got anything else down there?"

Outside, at the bar, Jack was still interviewing Terry and feeling good about the information he'd gotten so far. "Anybody else with the bikers?" he wanted to know.

"They came in, just the three of them. But there was this skinny black guy. . . . The oldest one was talkin' to this black guy."

Jack didn't allow his excitement to show as he unfolded the composite picture of Burroughs that he'd developed on the computer. "Something like this?" he asked.

She recognized him immediately. "Yeah, that's him. He didn't bother me. He was okay."

"Good. Thanks," Jack told her. "We need all the help we can get."

He turned to go, but Terry grabbed his arm. "I'll tell you something," she said. "This guy that grabbed me is one sick dude. I'm serious. I run into a lot of scumbags in here, but this one was . . . special. That's why I called you. This was a guy that should not be on the streets. He's bad news."

Jack couldn't agree with her more—and she didn't know the half of how special this guy was. He nodded at her and glanced around for Reggie, who'd disappeared.

That was no surprise. It was a safe bet the guy had zeroed in on some poor, unsuspecting girl and was now huddled in a corner, feeding her empty promises while squeezing her tits. Trust Reggie to conveniently forget that they were here on business.

In search of his partner, Jack wandered over to the bandstand. He was congratulating himself on the realization that he hadn't even been tempted to order a drink when he heard his name being called by someone in the crowd.

"Jack Cates!" boomed a voice behind him.

Jack turned and found himself face to face with a beefy, barrel-chested thug who was flanked by two equally oversized goons.

"Remember me?" the man snarled drunkenly.

"Yeah, sure," said Cates, grimacing as he was assailed by whiskey fumes. "You're the dumb son-of-a-bitch I busted for bein' in the backseat of a stolen Camaro with your pants down and a fifteen-year-old girl for a partner."

"I didn't steal that car. My buddy did."

"Pick better friends," Cates told him. As he recalled, the man had used the same excuse in court. The judge hadn't bought it then. Why should he believe it now?

"I got two years," the thug reminded him.

"Tough shit," Jack growled, trying to push his way past. "I'm in a hurry."

But the man had waited too long for this moment to let Cates go without extracting his full measure of revenge. Grabbing Jack by the elbow, he said, "I saw you on TV. You're not a cop anymore. You're suspended, right?"

"I'll see you later. I'm busy," said Jack, taking a step forward.

The thug grabbed Cates by the lapels of his jacket. "I got a lot to talk to you about, Cates," he blustered.

The guy had crossed the line from being a mild annoyance to a major pain in the ass, and he'd caught

Cates on a day when his patience was in particularly short supply.

"Aw, c'mon, give me a break. I don't want to get into any goddamned bar fights, and I don't want to hassle with somebody I collared. Looks bad on my record. Besides, people always get in fights in bars. It's a cliché. You hear about it all the time . . . hittin' people with bottles, knockin' 'em over chairs . . ."

By way of demonstration, Cates grabbed a bottle in one hand, a chair in the other, and smashed the thug in the face and head with a one-two punch. The man fell to the floor with a thud. Blood trickling down his forehead, he stared venomously at Cates as his friends hauled him to his feet.

"You blew it," Cates said, rubbing his sore shoulder. "I only need one arm to take care of a shit like you."

But the thug had plenty of fight left in him. Lunging forward, he swung a wide roundhouse that barely missed Cates's head. Jack ducked under the guy's fist and danced toward him. With his good arm, he belted an uppercut at the other man's chin. The thug howled with rage and staggered backward into the knot of screaming, cheering spectators.

Drawn by the noise, Reggie hurried back to the bar in time to catch Jack landing his second punch.

"I'm callin' the cops!" yelled Terry.

"Don't bother!" Reggie yelled back at her. "He *is* the cops!"

He watched as Cates moved in and tried to finish the fight with another quick punch to his opponent's head. The thug reeled from the blow but quickly recovered. He slammed a sharp hook into Cates's solar plexus, knocking the wind out of him. Beer bottles went flying as Cates slid backward across a table. He landed head first, showered with broken glass, in front of Reggie.

"How ya doin'?" Reggie asked.

"Great. I got 'im on the ropes." Jack grunted and scrambled to his feet.

Reggie chuckled. "Yeah. I can see that, man."

But his smile faded as the thug charged forward, bellowing like a wounded rhinoceros. Shaking off slivers of glass, Cates sidestepped him, aimed a kick at the man's groin—and missed. He was luckier the next time, connecting with the thug's head with two powerful punches.

By now, however, his assailant's goons had decided that they wanted a piece of the action. Grabbing Cates by the arms, they shoved him in front of their friend, who got ready to finish him off.

"I'm taking my two years outta your ass!" he roared. He reared back, wound up like a pitcher about to deliver a blazing fastball, and clobbered Cates with a volley of blows to his head and chest.

Seeing Jack doubled over with pain, Reggie decided it was time for him to jump into the act. "You got a gun under here?" he demanded of Terry.

"What?" She played dumb.

"A gun! For when you're gettin' robbed!"

"Yeah," she admitted, "but—"

"Gimme it!"

"I don't think—"

"Just gimme the goddamned gun!" he screamed. "You want to get him killed?"

Convinced that he wasn't going to take no for an answer, Terry pulled a pistol out of the cigar box, where it usually lay hidden, and handed it over.

Brandishing the gun in the air, Reggie hopped on top of the bar and fired it at the ceiling.

In case the goons hadn't gotten his point, he fired again—and once more after that for good measure.

The room went quiet. The fight came to a sudden halt.

Satisfied that he had the audience's attention, Reggie shouted, "Okay! Knock this shit off right now! Gotta tell you people, this has been a *bad* day for me. Got out of jail this morning. Since then I been shot at, hit by a big-ass truck, and somebody blew up my Porsche. Then tonight, right here, some bitch tries cuttin' my ass with a switchblade."

As he ticked off his list of grievances, Reggie became increasingly indignant about the pathetic welcome-home reception he'd received.

"I wait years to get out of jail," he continued, his voice rising angrily, "and I come back to this shit? Now, ordinarily, if some guys wanna kick the crap out of Jack Cates, I got no problem with it. But it just so happens I got a job to do with this guy, and he's got my money. So you better knock this whole thing off. Okay?"

"Because you got a gun?" yelled one of the goons.

"Damned right."

"Yeah?" The man snickered. "Well, I don't think you got the guts to use it."

That was all Reggie needed to hear. Without a second's hesitation, he pulled the trigger and shot the goon in the foot.

"Owww!" he howled.

His buddies quickly backed off.

"Fight's over," Reggie announced. He handed the pistol back to Terry. "Thank you."

"Let's go, Jack," he said, straightening his tie and preparing to leave.

Unfortunately, Jack Cates was not one to leave well enough alone. He'd yet to walk away from a situation without getting in his last licks. Reggie was already heading for the door when Cates slammed his head into the thug, then followed up with a stunning right-hand blow to his jaw.

"Shit!" Reggie muttered, watching the big man fold.

The man staggered to his feet. But Jack was there waiting for him with two overhand rights that sent him careening into a metal post. Just to make sure the decision was unanimous, Jack bounced the thug's head against the pillar a time or two until the fellow slid to the floor, down for the count.

One of his pals made a move for Jack. But Reggie took care of him with a flurry of fast, hard punches that ended with the goon slumped next to his boss. The other tough, who had his own personal bone to pick with Reggie on account of the bullet in his foot, limped up to smash Reggie over the head with a bar stool.

"Banzai!" Reggie screamed, and dispatched him with a well-placed heel to his wounded foot.

His victory was short-lived, however. Reggie was caught off guard as the first thug charged forward. Pinning Reggie against the bar, he yanked him by the throat and began to strangle him. Reggie grabbed for the overhead glass holder. The thug's hands were still around his throat when the wooden structure came crashing down on his head, knocking him unconscious.

Reggie panted and stared first at the pile of bodies, then at Cates.

"Smooth move, Jack," he said sarcastically.

"I hate bar fights," Jack groused as they walked out of the bar. "Where were you?"

"I had to go to the ladies' room."

"What?" Had Reggie made it with some girl in one of the bathroom stalls?

"Then after I got my business done, I had to save your ass," Reggie reminded him, in case Jack had forgotten who'd done most of the work just now.

"Thanks. But I didn't need your help," Jack threw back at him.

"I wasn't helping you. I was protecting my money," Reggie said, angrily clarifying the matter.

How could he have forgotten? Jack Cates never needed anybody's help. He was a loner . . . a hot dog . . . the kind of guy who flunked "ability to work well with others" in grade school. There probably wasn't a guy in his department who wanted to work with him. No wonder he'd come begging Reggie to help him out.

Well, from there on in, Cates had better watch his step. As far as Reggie was concerned, Jack was strictly on probation. One false move, and he'd see his dreams of finding the Iceman disappearing faster than an ice-cream cone in August.

9

Totally unaware of Reggie's anger and resentment, Jack unlocked the trunk of his car and began rummaging through all the junk that had accumulated there.

"I shoulda known this wasn't gonna be easy," he muttered, pushing aside a pile of dirty rags and a completely flat spare tire.

It took a while before he found what he was looking for—a battered metal box that opened with a creak to reveal a four-inch .44 Magnum.

"I always keep a spare handy. That fight in there shows what can happen to a fella if he's not carryin' a gun to protect himself," he explained, slipping the gun into his shoulder holster. "Say, Reggie?"

Reggie looked up, expecting an apology. "What?"

With his left hand, Cates slammed the trunk shut. With his right hand, he slammed Reggie in the face, knocking him to the pavement.

"What the fuck?" yelled Reggie, his face contorted with rage as he stared up at Cates.

"That's for the basketball. Now we're even," Jack calmly informed him.

"Even? Screw you! Deal's off." Reggie picked himself up off the sidewalk, shot Cates a look of pure hatred, and took off down the street.

Cates was stunned. What did he mean, the deal was off? Over one punch? Couldn't the guy take one punch without going crazy? "Reggie, where ya goin'?" he shouted after him. "What—Aw, shit . . ."

He quickly got into the car, threw it into Drive, and easily caught up with Reggie. Slowing down, he crawled alongside as Reggie marched at a brisk pace.

Reggie felt as if steam were coming out of his ears. Good thing he didn't have a gun, or he might have used it on Cates. Pretending to ignore his presence, Reggie kept on walking. But it was hard to keep the baby-blue Caddy out of his line of vision.

Finally, the pressure of his fury was too great to contain. "What the hell is wrong with you, Jack?" he exploded. "Were you born a shithead, or did you take some kinda lesson?"

Cates breathed a sigh of relief. He really thought he'd blown it this time. "Come on, Reggie, you're taking this too personal!" he shouted. "I just had to get even. That's the way I am. Now get in the car."

Reggie wasn't about to be so easily appeased. Cates was going to have to grovel—and sound sincere—before he would go anywhere near that car, let alone set his ass down on the seat. "Just get the fuck away from me. I told you before, I've had it with you. This time I mean it," Reggie said coldly.

"Don't be stupid. This is embarrassing. Where are you going?"

"Anywhere far away from you."

"Come on, Reggie, workin' with me's the best chance you got of stayin' alive," said Jack, altering his tactics.

"Then I'm better off dead," Reggie shot back.

"You wouldn't want to be buried in that suit," Cates told him, getting into the spirit of the dialogue.

"I can't buy me a new one. Some big, dumb asshole's got all my money. How do I know you even got my money?" Reggie demanded.

Cates shrugged. "Guess you have to trust me."

Reggie glared at him. "Good-bye," he declared. *Trust* him? Later for that, Jack.

"Look, your tip turned out okay," said Jack, trying to reason with him. "Ganz's old lady lives down in the Tenderloin. King Mei Hotel."

But Reggie didn't rise to the bait. As far as he was concerned, their partnership was over. And he wanted to make sure Cates knew they had reached the end of the line.

As he turned to go, he declared, "Good-bye. Kiss my ass. Good-bye."

Without waiting for Cates's reply, he calmly walked away.

Jack knew he'd pushed Reggie too far. But he couldn't wait around for the stupid son-of-a-bitch to come to his senses. Time was running out on him, and he needed to get some information fast. It looked as if he'd have to find the Iceman on his own.

Stopping at the nearest phone booth, he dropped a

quarter in the slot and dialed police headquarters. "Gimme Kehoe," he growled to the cop at the other end of the phone.

When Kehoe picked up the receiver and said hello, Jack greeted him with a perfunctory "Hey, Ben. How ya' doing?" Then he got right down to business. "You got anything for me yet?"

"Yeah," said Kehoe, who'd just been glancing over a computer printout.

"All right, give it to me," Jack demanded.

"Ganz, Richard. AKA 'Cherry,'" Kehoe read from the sheet. "Known member 'Western Brotherhood' motorcycle gang. Seven warrants. Seventy-two outstanding traffic violations."

"L.A. bike gangs?" Jack wanted to know.

"Yeah, L.A.P.D. faxed some stuff up a few minutes ago. Whole lot of shit."

Jack quickly digested the information. Then he said, "All right. I'll be right over."

"Jack—"

"Yeah?"

"Coming to the station ain't such a good idea," Kehoe told him. "Wilson's looking for you."

"Aw, Christ," Jack grumbled. "He heard about the bar. I didn't shoot anybody. Somebody else shot him. I just got in a damn fight. Grab everything you've got and be out front in fifteen minutes. Fifteen minutes, you got it?"

He hung up before Kehoe got in another word.

When Jack screeched to a halt in front of the station house exactly fifteen minutes later, Kehoe was standing there, nervously puffing on a cigarette, a manila folder tucked under his arm.

"Get in," Jack said by way of greeting.

Kehoe stubbed out the cigarette and climbed into the car.

"Whaddaya got?" Jack asked inelegantly.

"Are you nuts?" Kehoe glanced over his shoulder at the station house. "We can't sit out in front of the station. Wilson's right inside—"

Jack was getting awfully tired of having Wilson thrown up to him every five minutes. He wasn't worried. So what the hell was wrong with Kehoe and Cruise? With an exasperated sigh, he shoved his foot down on the gas pedal and roared away from the curb.

"You shouldn't have taken off after that show in the Tenderloin. Wilson's gone apeshit. Completely apeshit," Kehoe told him.

"That figures." Jack lit a cigarette and changed the subject. "What do you got for me?"

Kehoe opened the folder and waved it at Cates.

"Steer," said Jack, grabbing the file and pulling out a couple of prison I.D. photos. He recognized the faces. "Hickok and Ganz."

"This guy's Albert Ganz's brother—"

"Yeah," Jack interrupted. "I know about that."

Kehoe looked surprised but didn't bother asking Cates how he knew. His hands still on the wheel, he said, "Well, did you know that they're cop-killers? Capped two cops and a bystander five days ago. I talked to this Special Investigations guy in L.A. He says these guys are the enforcers for their gang, the Western Brotherhood. Last two years they've been linked to over fifteen deaths."

"Biker hit squad," Jack mused aloud.

"They take this shit very serious," Kehoe said. "Brake. *Brake!*" he screamed as they came within a couple of feet of rear-ending a car that was parallel parking.

Jack slammed on the brakes. Kehoe twisted hard on the steering wheel. The Caddy swerved out of range of the other car. Ahead of them, traffic was at a standstill because a construction crew was tearing up sections of the road. Cursing loudly, Jack grabbed the wheel, shifted into reverse, and began backing the wrong way down a one-way street.

Horns honked, and a couple of pedestrians shouted at him as he sped backward down the street.

Kehoe clutched at his seat until they reached the end of the block. He waited until Cates had thrown the car into Forward again. Then he continued to try to impress upon his friend the danger he was in.

"Jack," he said, wiping beads of perspiration off his brow, "these slime balls would take down a cop over a traffic ticket, and you killed this guy's brother. That mean's they're gonna come after you. Hard."

"So?" Jack hung a right, circling back toward the station house.

"So I don't want you to take any chances bringing these guys in. If you come up against these scumbags again, forget the Miranda. Blow their fuckin' heads off—"

"Hell of a way to talk to a cop on suspension, Ben."

"Fuck suspension. You're my friend," Kehoe said earnestly. "I wanna see you live a little longer."

Jack squealed to a stop in front of the precinct.

"Besides," Kehoe assured him, "shit you're in don't get any deeper. You're up to your neck."

Jack was about to thank him for his morale-boosting speech when Wilson came bounding out of the building. "Park the car, Cates!" he thundered, his cheeks flushed scarlet. He stopped short of throwing himself in front of the Caddy and roared, "Get upstairs, Kehoe. I'll talk to you later."

Kehoe glanced at Cates, then jumped out of the car, scurried up the sidewalk, and disappeared into the building like a scared rabbit.

Wilson strode over to the driver's side of the car and planted himself inches away from Cates's face. He leaned in so closely that Jack could see one of his eyelids twitching with tension.

"You crossed the line, Cates," he said, his voice thick with scorn. "After your involvement at this gunfight at the King Mei Hotel, and this barroom brawl we got a report on—you'll *never* be a cop again. You're totally out of control. Twenty-four hours from now I'm going to have to walk into that courtroom and close the book on you. And you know the sad part of it?" he demanded, pointing his finger for emphasis. "You helped me do it."

He paused for breath and momentarily backed off. Jack seized the opportunity. He shifted into drive, gunned the motor, and tore off down the street.

Though it was still early in the evening, the Tenderloin already throbbed with the tawdry sights and sounds of sex for sale. Overhead neon signs winked at passersby, tempting them with promises of "XXX! ALL NUDE! XXX!" Street-corner preachers shouted their messages of salvation, competing with the peddlers who raucously advertised their wares—everything from trays of stolen watches and rings to incense sticks and religious medals.

Potential customers sauntered down the crowded street, casting appraising glances at the porno bookstores, topless nightclubs, and X-rated movie theaters that had drawn them to the district. The newcomers looked nervous and furtive as they darted into the doorways of their choice. The regulars, some of whom lived in the area, stopped to rap with the vendors before moving on in search of titillation.

The Tenderloin had its peculiar gaudy charm, and Jack knew it well. Tonight, however, he was all business as he cruised the street, looking for the King Mei Hotel.

He found it without too much trouble. It was a run-down brick building with a flickering neon sign and a cardboard poster in the front window that said VACANCY in English and Chinese. Jack slammed on the brakes, narrowly missing a garbage truck that was picking up trash from a dumpster in the side alley. He parked the car in front of the hotel, got out, and walked up the stairs into the hotel.

The lobby consisted of two ratty armchairs and a listing coffee table whose surface was covered with scratches and cigarette burns. Sprawled in one of the chairs was an ancient, wrinkled Chinese man, either dead or passed out.

Glancing around, Jack spotted Reggie, smiling at him from across the room.

"Pretty nice place, huh, Jack? What took you so long?" asked Reggie.

"I thought you quit, for the fifth time," Jack said sourly.

Reggie shrugged.

"Couldn't stay away, huh, Reggie?" Jack said sarcastically. "Can't live without me."

"Look, I didn't sit in jail for another five years to

come out broke, or to get all shot up by a bunch of crazy-ass white trash bikers working for some piece of shit drug dealer, all right," Reggie retorted angrily.

"Admit it," Jack growled. "You *need* me."

"I'm gonna hang, Jack." Reggie's eyes glinted with fury as he laced into Jack. "We're gonna fix this shit. But I'm telling you, the next time you hit me, if you grab me, if you touch me too hard, if you look at me the wrong way—I'm gonna kill you!"

Cates laughed.

Reggie continued. "All right, man? I'm serious Jack. I'm gonna kill you."

"All right," Jack agreed, as Reggie crossed the room to join him. "Okay, Okay. I'm gonna treat you right."

"The only reason I'm putting up with your shit is 'cause I know you're in a lot of pain because you got bucked. What is it, your left arm fucked up?" Reggie asked, sounding sympathetic.

Jack appreciated his interest. "Yeah, yeah. It hurts like hell. Doc said it's bruised down to the bone."

Reggie was smiling solicitously as he hauled off and slugged Cates in his sore shoulder.

"Owww!" Jack yowled.

"Now we're even," Reggie said smugly.

"What about the basketball?" demanded Jack, grimacing with pain.

"You give me money back, and I'll let you throw a basketball in my face, okay? Now let's go to work."

"Look," Jack said, as they walked over to the front desk. "In case she's here, we're just going in to question the girl. This is straight-ahead cop stuff. Don't screw around."

Reggie threw him a dirty look. As usual, Cates was

sounding off to the wrong person. It was clear to Reggie which of them deserved the title of "most likely to mess up a sure thing."

"Spare me," he told Cates.

The reception area was covered from floor to ceiling by a smudged plexiglass shield. The two clerks, a Chinese couple, were barely visible behind the grill that was set into the shield.

"We wanna see a girl that lives here—name of Angel," said Cates, rapping on the plastic window.

The man lowered his Chinese-language newspaper and looked at the woman. They chatted briefly in Chinese, with the woman seemingly translating Cates's request. Then she said, "We never hear of her."

Jack flashed his toy badge. "Hear of her now?"

There was more conversation in Chinese between the couple. "That fake badge," the woman said dismissively. "My kid got one of those."

"Your kid got one of these?" Jack pulled open his jacket, revealing his .44.

The man spoke sharply to the woman. Apparently he'd suddenly remembered that Angel's name sounded familiar.

"Angel," said the woman, eyeing the gun respectfully. "Upstairs. Fourth floor. Four-B. Stair at back. Room on right."

Jack nodded. "Thanks. You got an elevator?"

"No! No! Busted. Stair only way up."

"Look, don't phone her, okay?" Jack told her. "Unless you want a lot of trouble. We'd like to surprise her."

The woman nodded and pointed them in the direction of a narrow corridor that was dimly let by an occasional bare bulb dangling overhead. She was all for surprises, so long as she wasn't on the receiving end.

Cherry's cycle rumbled around the corner and slowed to a stop a short distance away from the King Mei. Directly in front of the hotel, a police cruiser, its lights flashing, had just pulled over a souped-up '32 Deuce hot rod that had been doing sixty in a twenty-five-mile-an-hour zone.

As the cop got out of the patrol car and walked over to the Deuce, Cherry thought better of going in through the front door of the hotel. Gunning his engine, he rolled across the street and pulled into a darkened alleyway.

While Reggie and Jack walked down the hall toward the stairs, Jack prepared himself for disappointment. "Chances are she probably hasn't even seen the guy recently," he mused aloud. "He's in town for a hit, and he's not likely gonna take the time to pop his old girlfriend."

"No, he'd give her to his partner," Reggie retorted.

"What? Bullshit!"

"I'm serious. You don't know how these biker types think, Jack. Guy's got a hot chick, he likes to spread her around. Share the fun. They're like Eskimos."

They were halfway down the corridor when Reggie was distracted by a whirring noise coming from behind a piece of thick black drapery. He cautiously pulled back the curtain and liked what he saw there: an old Chinese man was applying a colorful dragon tattoo to the breast of a young Oriental girl. The girl gazed up at Reggie with half-lidded, opium-clouded eyes.

"Jack, I know what I want for Christmas," he said, licking his lips.

Jack pulled him away from the curtain and pushed him toward the stairs. "Get a grip, Reggie," he ordered.

"Jack, it's been five years. That's the problem. All I been doin' is grippin' myself."

Ignoring Reggie's last comment, Jack peered up the empty stairwell. "You wait here on the landing, and I'll go up and see the lady," he said.

"Wrong," Reggie informed him, having already figured out the strategy. "I ain't got a gun. You wait down here. I don't want those bikers coming up behind me when all I can whip out is my dick. If she's there, I'll give you a shout."

Jack decided that made sense. "Okay. You want the badge?"

"No, thanks, man. I don't think I'm gonna run into any little kids on the way up." Reggie chuckled quietly as he headed up the stairs.

Cates watched him go and hoped he hadn't made a mistake. Leaning against the wall, he discovered that next to his head was a window covered with black cardboard. He peeled away one of the corners and looked out at a garbage-strewn alley. It was empty except for the row of huge dumpsters on the far side.

Disappointed not to find any bikers lurking behind the building, Cates lit up a cigarette and settled back to wait for Reggie.

* * *

Cherry's headlights shone on Hickok's Harley, hidden from view beneath the hotel's fire escape. Cherry parked his Harley right behind Hickok's. Then he balanced himself on the seat of his bike, reached up, and quietly pulled down the metal fire-escape ladder.

Cherry's girlfriend, Angel, lay in bed with the sheet pulled up as far as her tattooed shoulders. "When's Cherry coming over?" she asked Hickok, who was pulling on his jeans.

"Don't worry about it. He'll be by," Hickok assured her.

Angel pouted. She'd been hoping for company, but Hickok had hopped out of the sack as soon as he'd finished with her.

Hickok grinned as he pulled on his gloves. "He told me you were real nice. He was right."

Suddenly there was a loud knock on the door. Hickok grabbed his revolver and glanced questioningly at Angel.

She shrugged. It couldn't be Cherry. He wouldn't bother to knock. Her bills were all paid up, and she wasn't expecting any visitors. "Yeah? Who is it?" she yelled.

"Pizza delivery."

"I didn't order any," she yelled.

"Pizza delivery for room forty-two. Angel," the man shouted back.

Hickok nodded at her to open the door. She climbed out of bed and began pulling on a filmy kimono that did little to hide her nakedness. "Hold on, I got to get dressed," she called. Lowering her voice, she said to Hickok, "I didn't order any pizza."

On the other side of the door, Reggie muttered to himself, "Get dressed? Maybe we better check this out." He bent down to look through the keyhole just as Hickok fanned his .45 and began blasting the door with a hail of bullets.

The wooden door exploded in splinters. Reggie made a fast dive for shelter.

Cates grabbed his gun and raced up the stairs, taking them two at a time. Cherry, who by now had crawled through a window and reached the third floor corridor, pulled out his automatic and made a dash for the stairs.

In the lobby, the Chinese couple heard the gunshots and began arguing about what to do. The woman pointed to the phone, then ran down the hall that led to the stairs.

Hickok pulled open the blasted door. He looked left and right, but the hallway was open. Quickly reloading his gun, he moved carefully along the wall.

"Where you goin'?" Angel shouted after him. "What's goin' on?"

Cherry had gotten as far as the third floor landing when Cates came running up the stairs. They both started firing at the same moment. Bullets ricocheted off the wall. Windows shattered. Thick clouds of plaster dust flew into the air, mixing with the gunsmoke.

Cates ducked into a crouch and dove down the stairs. Cherry pulled back to the corridor. Cates edged around the corner and blasted two shots.

Cherry let go with two of his own, screaming, "I killed you! I already killed you!"

He was still blasting his automatic when Jack

caught sight of the woman clerk, on the stairwell below him, screaming at him in Chinese.

"Get back! Call for help!" Jack roared. "Call for help! Call for police! Do it now!"

On the floor above him, Hickok crept along the hallway, looking for the would-be intruder. A door opened and a man appeared. Hickok didn't stop to ask questions before he opened fire. The man died in mid-scream as Hickok's bullets blew out the front of his chest. Fountains of blood sprayed all over the wall and floor.

Hickok threw himself into the room. Reggie was waiting for him. He kicked Hickok in the groin, then threw a punch to his nose. Hickok dropped his gun, and Reggie dived for it. Unarmed, Hickok jumped up and raced back down the corridor, with Reggie right on his heels.

Reggie leveled the gun and was about to fire when Angel suddenly jumped into his sight line.

"No, don't! Don't do it!" she screamed. "Don't shoot!"

Reggie knocked her aside and took off after Hickok.

Down a flight, Cherry was taking aim at Cates. "You killed my family!" he yelled, and fired twice.

Cates blasted two back at him.

As the gunshots reverberated through the hotel, Hickok tore into one of the rooms, slammed the door, and grabbed a piece of conduit off the wall. Reggie raced in after him, and Hickok swung at him, barely missing Reggie's head. Then he tore out of the room and down the stairs.

"Cherry!" he shouted.

Cherry turned, looked up the stairs, and slammed

three slugs at Reggie. Glass and wooden splinters exploded in his face. Cherry blasted two more rounds at Reggie and Jack. Then he and Hickok leaped out the third-story window, onto the fire escape.

The bikers were already one flight down by the time Cates and Reggie reached the open window. Reggie fired twice. Dodging his bullets, Hickok and Cherry hopped onto the fire-escape railing and jumped. They landed in the garbage dumpsters parked three stories below in the alley.

"Down!" roared Cates. He hurled himself down the stairs, with Reggie right on his heels.

Hickok and Cherry, meanwhile, had jumped on their bikes and wheeled around in a spray of gravel. They zoomed up the alley, roared around the corner, and slammed on their brakes. The garbage truck that had been parked earlier in front of the hotel now completely blocked their only exit.

Hickok made a circle in the air with his finger, signaling Cherry to turn around and follow him. They accelerated and tore back down the alley. Their bikes were doing about a hundred miles an hour by the time they reached the far side of the alley, which butted up against a brick wall, inset by a window set low to the ground.

Hickok pulled a wheelie. With Cherry at his side, he burst through the window, then tore through the worn movie screen in front of it. The theater patrons watched in stunned amazement as the two bikes emerged between the spread legs of a porn star. They raced up the aisle to the lobby and crashed through the theater's glass front doors.

Cates and Reggie burst out of the hotel just as the bikers were headed up the block past the King Mei.

They raised their guns, aimed . . . and almost opened fire on a trolley car full of screaming Japanese businessmen.

Cherry and Hickok careened around the far side of the trolley and disappeared from view. The sound of their bikes faded into the distance.

"Shit!" said Reggie, looking disgusted.

Cates silently echoed his sentiments, as he relieved Reggie of his gun and lit a cigarette.

Jack was huddled with Reggie and Cruise around a police car parked down the street from the King Mei. The block behind them was crawling with squad cars, ambulances, and paddy wagons. He strained to hear Kehoe above the noise and confusion of the crime-scene experts, medical attendants, plainclothes officers, and news reporters.

Clutching a mobile cellular phone to his ear, Cruise was talking to someone back at the station house. "We got the perimeter secure. No, Jack's okay," he was saying. "I don't know. I don't know. Haven't had a chance to get a statement from him yet. I don't know whose gun he used. I'll get a statement. Sure. Okay."

Cruise shook his head as he hung up the phone. "You're in deep shit, Jack," he said.

"Tell me something I don't know."

Cruise had more bad news for Jack. He pulled Burrough's mug shot out of his pocket. "I already ran this guy through N.C.I.C. Couldn't get a match."

"Christ!" Jack exclaimed. "Give me a break!"

10

Dense clouds of steam hung in the air of the prison shower room. Rivers of moisture rolled down the sides of the green-tiled walls. In the locker room just outside the shower area, a crowd of naked cons, skimpy gray towels wrapped around their waists, impatiently waited their turn. They could hear the steady stream of water splashing in the twenty-faucet shower stall next door. The water was hot now, but it would feel icy-cold against the skin of those unfortunate enough to be standing at the end of the line.

Kirkland Smith never had to worry about cold water. As part of the bargain he'd struck long ago with the guards, he had the right to shower first—and in private. In return, he kept the peace in the blocks adjacent to his cell. Granting Smith special privileges was a small price to pay for a quiet, trouble-free prison.

Usually Kirkland hated to be interrupted while he was showering. But tonight he couldn't relax. He was waiting to hear about the money.

He was soaping himself up when the guard stuck his head in the stall and shouted, "Smith!"

"What?" Kirkland yelled above the hiss of the water.

"That call you were expecting. The money man!"

Kirkland acknowledged the guard with a grunt. He grabbed his towel from a hook on the wall and wiped his face. The cons outside gave him a wide berth as he pushed past, the water still dripping from his thickly muscled body.

He picked up the phone at the hallway guard station and right away said, "Reggie?"

Reggie was calling from a phone booth in North Beach. "Yeah, it's me—"

"You got it done?"

"It's more complicated than that—" Reggie tried to explain.

Kirkland didn't need to be called away from a hot shower in order to be told about complications. He didn't want excuses. He wanted action. He'd been warned about Reggie Hammond, but he'd gone ahead and taken a chance on him. Kirkland didn't appreciate finding out he'd made the wrong decision. Nor did he like having to waste his resources or call in favors to collect on an overdue debt.

"You been out a whole day and I'm not paid? Don't mess with me, Reggie!" he cautioned. "Remember, you ain't a citizen no more. You can't vote. Nobody'll hire your ass. You're an outcast. Nobody wants you. All that's left of Reggie Hammond is his word . . . You're breakin' your word, Reggie."

Kirkland didn't need to mention the consequences Reggie faced if he reneged on their deal. That was better left to Reggie's imagination. He slammed down the receiver and stomped off to finish his shower.

Reggie stared at the dead phone and mentally calculated how much time he had left before Smith sent out his goons. At the top of the plus column was Kirkland's desire to see a return on his investment. On the minus side was Kirkland's need to uphold his reputation. He couldn't afford to let it get around town that someone had welshed on him. The equation added up to one inescapable fact: Reggie was swimming in deep shit.

He glanced across the street, where Angel sat wrapped in a blanket in the backseat of a police cruiser. Tucking his tie into his jacket, he strolled over to have a chat with Cherry's girl.

Cruise saw him opening the car door and asked Cates, "Who's your friend?"

"An old pal," said Jack. "What about the girl?"

"She's not talking," said Cruise, who'd pressured her with every legal threat at his disposal.

She's not talking to you, Reggie would have corrected him if he'd heard Cruise's comment. He had no doubt that Angel would quickly succumb to *his* silver-tongued powers of persuasion. There was hardly a woman alive who could resist him when he poured on the charm.

Creasing his forehead with a show of concern, he slid into the seat next to Angel. "All right, honey," he said smoothly, "from where I'm sitting you're looking at accessory to murder one. That's at least five to ten years inside—even with good behavior. Now, if you want to cooperate, maybe you won't have to do any time at all."

Angel glared at him and pulled the blanket more tightly around her. She knew her rights, and this joker was stepping all over them. "I told the other cop. I got nothin' to say till I talk to a lawyer!" she spat.

But Reggie knew from the lines of tension bracketing her mouth that she wasn't as tough as she was pretending to be. It might take a while, but he would get something out of her.

He shrugged. "Okay, but I can tell you what time inside is going to do to a fine woman like you, locked up with all those bull dykes and starchy food . . ."

"You're scaring the shit outta me."

Reggie matched her sarcasm with a dose of his own. "I get it. It's love. Guy like Cherry Ganz, blowing into town once or twice a year, letting his friends jump up and down on you, beating the shit out of you when he's drunk—that's definitely worth going to jail to protect. You got to love the guy. I can see that."

He reached for the door handle.

"I don't know where they are," Angel said in a small voice.

Reggie saw the fear in her eyes and kept his face neutral.

"They move around all the time," she explained. "I can never get in touch with them."

"Who can?"

"Just . . . I don't know . . ." She shivered. "These guys are nuts."

"Don't worry—"

His attempt to assure her was interrupted as the front door was suddenly yanked open. Cates poked his head in the car and stared at them across the backseat.

Angela jumped, and Reggie didn't miss a beat. "Good. Officer Cates," he said briskly, "get in here and get your notebook out."

Jack threw him a look: *Are you nuts?* He opened his mouth, but Reggie cut him off.

"Miss Allen has decided to cooperate with the investigation." He arched his eyebrow, a signal to Cates: *Don't blow this, pal.* Then he prompted the girl: "Now, Angel, you were going to tell me who Cherry's contact man is . . . Cates! Take this down!"

"Yeah . . . uh . . . right, Inspector Hammond," Cates mumbled, gritting his teeth and pulling out his notebook.

"Now, Angel . . ."

Angel picked at a cuticle and stared off into space. "The guy's name is Malcolm Price," she said. "Big guy, long hair. Spooky eyes. Nobody talks to Cherry unless they talk to him first."

"Where do we find him?" asked Reggie.

"I have no idea." She looked up at him pleadingly. "I swear. I only know a name."

Jack and Reggie exchanged glances. They obviously weren't going to get anything more out of Angel.

"Thanks, babe," said Reggie, opening the door and getting out of the car.

Jack didn't bother with a thank you. He was already out of the car and headed for the phone booth across the street. By the time Reggie caught up with him, Jack was going through the phone book, looking for Malcolm Price's name and number.

"That figures," he said disgustedly, snapping the phone book shut. "No listing."

"Jack, this is a biker, not an insurance agent,"

Reggie pointed out. "Bikers don't get listed in phone books."

"You gotta cover every angle. That's what police work is, Reggie. A lot of details. That's how we catch guys like you," Jack shot back. He glanced at Reggie alongside him and chuckled briefly. "You know, the next time you impersonate a cop, you ought to change clothes. No detective would be caught dead in that outfit."

"You're right, Jack." Reggie nodded his agreement. "If I want to pretend I'm a cop, I'll buy myself a cheap-ass suit and hang out at a doughnut stand."

Cruise was leaning against the Caddy, waiting for Jack. As he and Reggie got into the car, Jack issued instructions to Cruise. "Radio back to Kehoe and tell him to run up an address on this Malcolm Price guy. Tell him to have it for me by the time I get there. We're outta here."

"Wait a minute!" Cruise protested. "You can't just take off! You got to make a statement."

But he was too late. Jack was already pulling away from the curb. As the Caddy zoomed off down the street, Cruise shouted, "Come on, Jack! Your ass is gonna be grass!"

Jack and Reggie drove up Broadway for about a mile without saying a word. Finally, Reggie broke the silence.

"Hey, Jack, how long before your boys find out an address on Price?" he asked.

Jack turned left, though he wasn't exactly sure in what direction they were headed. "It's hard to say. They're workin' on it."

"At the rate we're going, you're gonna pick up Price at my funeral."

"Aw, don't worry about your funeral. If the Iceman gets you, we won't even find your body."

Reggie was beginning to have a problem with Cates's attitude. His crack about the Iceman was too close to the truth to be funny. It was only a matter of hours before Cates would be permanently out of a job—and Reggie could be permanently out of a life. Somebody had to start digging up dirt on Price and Burroughs, and Reggie could see that the cops weren't up to the job.

"You know what the problem is, man? We need to go somewhere and talk to somebody who knows about stuff like this," he told Cates.

"Okay." Jack shrugged. He had no quarrel with that. "Where?"

"Honest?"

"Yeah."

Reggie inhaled deeply, filling his lungs with the night-sharpened air. The street around him crackled with the sounds and smells he loved best—the sounds and smells of the city, of people doing their thing. The whole time he'd been in jail, he'd dreamed of nights like this. But he might not be enjoying too many more of them, unless he and Cates could ice the Iceman.

Unfortunately, there was only one place to go for the information they needed.

"Back to prison," he told Cates.

"Aw, bullshit!" Jack growled.

"Hey, Jack, you got any better ideas on how to find out something about Price? I got a guy on the inside that knows everything about everybody. He can finger anybody. Plus you need to go back there anyway, 'cause you might be spending some time there real soon." Reggie chuckled. "I think it'd be good for you to go back and get reacquainted with some of the brothers whose rights you violated."

The tip of Jack's cigarette glowed in the darkness. "Aw, don't give me that shit. I just arrest crooks. I don't make them steal."

"Get the fuck out!" Reggie heatedly defended himself and his friends. "You make it sound like everybody went down to the guidance counselor, took a test, and the results came back that 'crook' was the only job they qualified for."

"Aw, that's real good, Reggie. Yeah, sure, blame society. Put it all on society's shoulders."

Reggie could see he was wasting his breath. Cates was a cop, with a cop's mentality. No use trying to teach him what it meant to have grown up in a slum where the only guys willing to give you a break were the drug dealers on the corner.

He yawned, loosened his tie, and made himself comfortable. "Let me tell you something, Jack," he said, closing his eyes. "If shit was worth something, poor people would be born with no assholes."

On a deserted street in another part of the city, a pay phone rang three times before it was answered by a thin black man in a raincoat.

"Yeah, it's me," said Burroughs, peering through the windows of the phone booth. ". . . I heard about it. I warned you about dealing with these crazy-ass crackers, man . . . What? No, I'm not carrying. That's not my thing. You know that. Look, I'm a businessman, too. I just do not want to get in their way, okay?

They take all the fun out of my work. . . . Yeah, I remember, it's just—I *said,* you don't have to remind me . . . Okay, don't worry, I'll put it together."

He hung up the phone without saying good-bye. Then he checked his watch, glanced up and down the block, and hurried into the night.

• 11

Cherry slammed his fist against the corrugated-steel wall of the Oakland warehouse where he was holed up with Hickok, watching the eleven o'clock news on television. "One lucky cop, one lucky nigger." He scowled at his pal.

Hickok ignored him. He was busy reloading his shotgun, thumbing the fat twelve-gauge rounds one by one into the drum magazine.

Cherry threw himself into the chair in front of the TV and glared at the anchorwoman who was reading the news.

"The stars turned out in force for the mayor's benefit to feed the homeless," she said brightly. "Luminaries from the arts, including television and motion-picture stars, were on hand for the posh thousand-dollar-a-plate affair. This, on the heels of stern criticism of the city government's closing of fourteen city-funded shelters this past December . . .

". . . The Tenderloin district exploded tonight in what authorities are calling one of the most violent days in northern California history," said the anchorman, moving on to her next story. "Sixteen police units and T.A.C. squad personnel responded to the scene of a gunfight between an off-duty police officer and an undisclosed number of motorcycle gang members. The shooting occurred at the King Mei Hotel on Broadway. This came just a few hours after two other biker-involved attacks on U.S. Highway Fifty . . ."

Cherry leaned forward in his chair as video footage appeared on the screen, showing the aftermath of the King Mei shootout. The camera panned from a shot of the dead man, splattered with blood, being carried on a gurney into an ambulance, to a closeup of Cates and Hammond leaving the crime scene.

Hickok looked down the length of his gun barrel. "Workin' for this Iceman of yours sucks," he said.

Cherry shrugged. "You ain't supposed to like it. You're just supposed to do it."

". . . the assailants engaged in the exchange of gunfire," the anchorwoman continued, "with San Francisco Police Department Inspector Jack Cates, a fifteen-year veteran of the police force, currently on suspension pending an investigation into the recent shooting incident at the motorcycle raceway at Hunter's Point."

Cherry had seen and heard about as much as he could take. He drew his gun, pointed it at the TV set, and blew out the screen. Pieces of glass shattered all over the floor.

The first golden rays of sunlight were just breaking over the craggy stone walls of the prison that Reggie Hammond had most recently called home. Inside the darkened cellblocks, some of the prisoners were already awake. Others tossed fitfully, trying to grab a few more minutes of sleep and solitude before the morning bell summoned them to another day behind bars.

In Block B, a door flung open. A guard walked into the cell where Kirkland Smith lay sleeping on his bunk. The guard glanced at Smith, then hammered his nightstick against the con's metal toilet. Smith sprang awake and was instantly alert. There was murder in his eyes.

"Let's go," said the guard. "You got some visitors."

The visiting area was a long, narrow room, divided down the middle by a thick wall of glass. On either side of the glass was a series of cubicles, each set off from the next by a waist-high metal barricade. Each cubicle consisted of a small wooden table, a couple of chairs, and a black telephone receiver that was attached to the wall.

The guard hadn't given Kirkland much time to get dressed. He was wearing the undershirt he'd slept in and a pair of work pants when he stepped into the visiting room.

"Shit!" he said when he saw who was waiting to talk to him on the other side of the glass partition. Settling himself into the chair, he picked up the phone receiver and eyed the white dude who had squeezed into the booth alongside Reggie Hammond.

"I'm impressed, Reggie," Kirkland said into the phone. "You came down here in person to tell me you paid off your debt, right?" He spoke loudly enough so that Jack could hear him, even though Reggie was holding the receiver.

Jack glanced from one man to the other. "What debt?" he wanted to know.

"There's been papers out on me ever since I got transferred over here. He's my protection. We got a deal," Reggie quickly explained. He leaned forward and answered Kirkland's question. "Not yet, but I'm not fucking with you. I got a problem."

Kirkland grunted with displeasure. "You got one big problem—me. And until you pay me off, we got nothin' to talk about." He nodded at Cates and asked, "Who's the cop?"

Reggie had been expecting this and was prepared to tell Kirkland the truth . . . or at least his version of it. With any luck, Cates would be smart enough to keep his mouth shut.

"He's okay," Reggie told Kirkland. "He's working for me."

Kirkland rolled his eyes. "You and a cop? Cut me some slack, man."

Jack was fed up with the back-and-forth between the two cons. Nor did he appreciate Reggie's bullshit about him. The sun was coming up and time was running short.

Grabbing the phone away from Reggie, he growled at Smith, "Look, I don't know what you two got going, and I don't give a shit. But if you don't help him help me . . . he's dead."

There was a momentary pause, almost if the connection had gone dead. Then Kirkland said, "What do you want, Reggie?"

"Who is the Iceman?"

Kirkland shrugged. "All I know is he's connected. Cops can't touch him."

Jack pulled out his mug shot of Burroughs and slammed it flat against the window. "What about this guy?"

"Small-time dealer by the name of Burroughs. Recruited by the Iceman a couple of months ago."

Burroughs's story was news to Reggie, but he didn't let it show. "The guy's trying to kill me," he told Kirkland. "They got a main man named Malcolm Price."

"I know him. Western Brotherhood. You want those boys for a hit, you gotta go through Price."

"Where's he at?" asked Reggie.

"Oakland. Does his business out of a motel on the Beltway. Has for years. Sunset Motel."

"Sunset Motel? You got an address?" asked Jack.

Kirkland felt pushed, and he didn't like the feeling. It went against his grain to be so free and easy with his facts, but it seemed the surest way to see the color of Reggie's money. The cop, however, owed him nothing—and vice versa. "Do I look like a fucking phone book?" he roared into the phone. "Sunset Motel on the Beltway. Look it up."

He leaned up to the glass and motioned to Reggie to do likewise. "Reggie," he said, "I gotta talk to you in private . . ."

Reggie moved closer to the window, away from Cates.

"Now that I have given you something you need for

a second time, Reggie," Kirkland said in a low, menacing voice that left no doubt as to his intentions, "you will repay your debt to me."

Kirkland reared back suddenly and crashed his fist through the partition, punching a large round hole in the glass. Jagged-edged chunks of glass flew into the air.

Jack and Reggie leaped up, ready to grab Smith, but the clanging alarm had already summoned the guards. They rushed in and jumped all over him.

"You ain't untouchable, Reggie!" Kirkland screamed as they dragged him out of the room. "Remember that! Don't you forget it!"

Joe Stevens was on duty at the squadroom message center desk that morning. When the phone rang, he wearily picked it up and said, "Stevens."

"Cap, it's me," said Jack, calling from the prison.

"Hiya, Jack. What's up?" asked Stevens.

"Listen, I'm in prison," Jack began.

"Really? I always said you'd come to a bad end," Stevens chuckled. "By the way, Wilson's looking for you again. He went ballistic when he heard about what happened at the King Mei."

"Aw, that dickhead ought to be a garbage collector."

"I'll send him your regards. You know this guy you're looking for? Price . . . that guy, Malcolm Price? We got a location on him," Stevens said.

Jack couldn't believe his luck was finally changing. "Great!" he told Stevens. "We're heading back for Oakland."

"Take your time, kiddo," said Stevens. "He ain't going nowhere."

* * *

The Oakland Police Morgue was in a concrete-walled basement lined with rows of white-sheeted gurneys that contained the coroner's works-in-progress. The cloyingly sweet smell of formaldehyde pervaded the atmosphere. Overhead fluorescent lights shone down mercilessly on stainless-steel banks of drawers, one of which slid open to reveal the very dead body of Malcolm Price.

"Must of been a real good lead, Jack. Somebody shot him sixteen times," Stevens said dryly.

Jack was feeling the cumulative effect of the last twenty-four hours. Exhausted and disheartened by this latest development, he muttered, "I've been busting my hump on this Iceman thing for years. Every time I get close . . . another goddamned dead end."

Stevens looked sympathetic. "Sorry, Jack. This job can drive you crazy," he said as he walked away.

Reggie was still staring at Price's body when a startling idea clicked into place. "The Iceman's a cop," he said quietly.

Jack glared at him. "A dirty cop?"

"Yeah!" Reggie snapped his fingers. "I'm talking filthy—even for a crook."

"Bullshit." Jack stuck his fists in his pockets. "No way."

"Come on, Jack, put this shit together, man. Think about it," Reggie said excitedly. "You ask for Price's address—and the Iceman shows up there first."

Jack shook his head. "Coincidence. Bad luck."

"It ain't no damn coincidence, Jack. What about the brother's pic you're waving around?"

Jack pulled out Burroughs's mug shot and handed it to Reggie.

"Nothing. That doesn't mean anything," Jack said

stubbornly. "We have to run the mug shot through N.C.I.C. It takes time to get a make."

"How long's that take?"

"Hours."

"It's been hours," Reggie pointed out.

"Sometimes it's slow," Jack replied, still resisting Reggie's dirty cop theory.

"Hey, Jack you're just making lame excuses," Reggie insisted. The mystery was becoming clearer to him by the second. "I'll tell you why the Iceman wants to kill me. It's got nothing whatsoever to do with this money. That's horseshit to him. He wants to kill me because I've seen him. I'm on the street, now he knows I can identify him. He thinks I'm gonna blow his cover or something. The same guy that's out to kill me, is the one who's fucking up your investigation."

"I thought about it once," Jack said reluctantly. "No . . . it doesn't add up."

"It does add up. You just don't want to admit it. Look, find the guy that's putting up the most resistance 'cause you're on the case. You'll probably find out that motherfucker's the Iceman."

A light bulb went off in Jack's head. "Wilson," he said. "That prick Wilson from Internal Affair's been dogging my ass for years. Ever since I started looking for the Iceman. All through this thing. You sure you can recognize him?" he asked Reggie.

"Yeah," Reggie assured him. "Big ugly white guy."

"Sounds right. If Wilson is the Iceman, then I gotta get you to that hearing, and you can ID him and—"

"What hearing?" Reggie interrupted.

"The one where they decide if they're gonna try and put me in jail and take away my badge for good," said Jack. He glanced at his watch. "It started about ten minutes ago."

He was going to be late for his own goddamned trial.

• 12

Two rows of uniformed police officers sat in the visitors' gallery of the first-floor state courtroom. Some of the officers, recently in from a midnight-to-eight shift, sat dozing as they waited for the proceedings to begin. A fellow cop's ass was on the line. Tired as they were, they wanted to lend him their support. Also present was a scattering of newspaper and television reporters. Jack Cates wasn't yet a headline grabber, but the potential was there.

The pretrial hearing was getting off to a late start. Though the judge was already present, the defendant, Jack Cates, was not. Cates's lawyer had approached the bench and pleaded with the judge to allow his client a few more minutes before His Honor called court into session. The judge had granted him a ten-minute grace period. Now, however, with Cates still a no-show, he banged his gavel and announced that it was time to call the first witness.

The district attorney stood up and said, "The state calls Inspector Ben Kehoe to the stand."

While Harry Bryant checked his watch and tried to look nonchalant, Kehoe walked slowly to the front of the courtroom and was sworn in.

The D.A. approached the witness stand. "Could you detail the events following the shooting at Hunter's Point Raceway?" he asked Kehoe.

Kehoe had hoped to talk to Cates before he testified. Now, looking out at the courtroom, he wondered what the hell had happened to him. Was there some new break in the case? And if so, why hadn't Cates shared it with him?

These questions were on his mind as he cleared his throat and answered, "Fifteen officers including myself searched the track for twelve hours."

"How exhaustive a search?"

"All the hay bales in the pit were opened, the hay sifted," Kehoe replied. "Oil-drainage grates in the pit were removed and searched with metal detectors. The infield dirt was cut and dragged with rakes."

"And no gun was found." The D.A. tapped his index finger against his lower lip, then continued. "Where were the track employees during this time? The pit mechanics, drivers, others?"

"They were kept outside of the roped-off area, once our units had arrived on the scene," Kehoe said, then took a sip of water.

The D.A. nodded thoughtfully. "Could any track employees have entered the pit area in the time between the shooting and the arrival of the backup officers?"

"Possibly. But Jack . . . uh . . . Inspector Cates . . . claims he had the crime scene closed off very soon after the event and kept it that way until we arrived. He said he hadn't touched anything after determining that the suspect was beyond his help."

"What was his attitude?"

"Huh?" Kehoe squinted quizzically at the D.A.

"How did he seem?"

"He was cool. I mean"—Kehoe shrugged—"he didn't seem particularly upset."

"Not particularly upset at having taken a life?" questioned the D.A., raising his voice to emphasize the last three words.

"I didn't mean that. I meant—" His face flushed, Kehoe searched for the right word. "He didn't seem traumatized."

The D.A. nodded. "No more questions, Mr. Kehoe," he said, dismissing him.

Kehoe stepped down from the witness box. There was still no sign of Cates. Even Jack wasn't dumb enough to skip out on his own hearing. Or was he? Kehoe wondered. He considered sticking around to find out, then decided against it and left the courtroom to return to the station house.

"The state calls Sergeant Frank Cruise," declared the district attorney.

Cruise would have preferred to be anywhere but this courtroom, but he hadn't been given a choice. He, too, was extremely curious as to Cates's whereabouts. His hands were sweaty with tension as the bailiff approached to swear him in.

While Cruise was promising to tell the whole truth and nothing but, Bryant glanced over his shoulder, hoping to see Cates come barreling through the door.

But he still hadn't appeared by the time the D.A. posed his first question to Cruise.

"Sergeant Cruise," he said, "how long have you been a San Francisco police officer?"

"Twelve years," replied Cruise, nervously twirling his pinky ring.

"And how long have you known Inspector Jack Cates?"

"Let's see . . . about eight years. And I'd like to say," he declared, turning to face the judge, "that he's about the finest officer I've ever worked with and the hardest-working—"

The judge glared at him and pounded his gavel. "Sergeant Cruise," he reprimanded the witness, "please confine your answers to the specifics of the question only. We're not interested in your editorializing."

"Yes, Your Honor," said Cruise, barely masking his resentment.

The D.A., aware that he was dealing with a defensive witness, briskly asked Sergeant Cruise to recall the facts pertaining to the incident at the raceway. Cruise's testimony was much the same as Kehoe's, and the D.A. soon told him he could step down.

His next witness was far more cooperative. Inspector Wilson was only too happy to review the events of the morning in question with the district attorney.

"And your office has had Inspector Cates under close observation ever since?" the D.A. noted.

"Yes." Wilson leaned forward in the witness stand and explained the genesis of his particular interest in Cates. "After an incident in the Mission District, Cates dredged up this theory of a criminal mastermind controlling drug traffic in the Bay area. For the last four years, he has, in my opinion, wasted the department's resources and manpower—risked officers' lives to vindicate himself and his theories."

"Can you describe the detective in question's professional attitude?" asked the D.A., obviously pleased with Wilson's response.

Wilson didn't have to be asked twice. He'd waited a long time for this moment. "Jack Cates is an anachronism," he responded, pressing his palms together and making a steeple of his fingers. "When a police officer takes it upon himself to violate department regulations and suspects' civil rights, it makes it hard on all the good cops who're trying to do their jobs."

Bryant jumped to his feet. "Objection, Your Honor. These remarks have nothing to do with the incident at hand."

"On the contrary, Your Honor," argued the D.A. "I'm trying to show a pattern of behavior on Inspector Cates's part that will illuminate the events at Hunter's Point."

The judge nodded. "I'll allow the testimony to stand."

"It's basic, Your Honor," Wilson earnestly elaborated further. "The difference between a good cop and a bad one. A good cop is someone who sees himself as a cog in a wheel . . . a public servant whose prime concern is the well-being of the average everyday citizen. A bad cop is one who feels justified in bending the law as he goes along."

The judge listened to the witnesses' testimonies, then called for a brief recess. He'd reconvened the session when the light blue Caddy lurched to a halt outside the courthouse. Cates and Hammond leaped out of the car and bounded up the steps. Reggie was his usual impeccably groomed self. Jack was combing his hair with his fingers and tucking in his shirt as he galloped down the corridor.

"In consideration of the preliminary evidence presented thus far by the state, and in adherence to the laws, statutes, and rules specified by the state of California, city of San Francisco, this court—" The judge was giving his ruling as Cates and Hammond burst through the courtroom door.

The spectators buzzed excitedly. A couple of cops broke out in cheers when they caught sight of Cates.

"Order! Please!" shouted the judge, pounding his gavel. "This is an official hearing. Let's have some order here! Who are these men?"

"That's Inspector Cates, Your Honor," the D.A. replied helpfully.

Panting and red-faced, Jack paid no attention to the judge's angry bellows. He quickly surveyed the room until he found his quarry, seated toward the front. "That him?" he demanded of Reggie, pointing at Wilson.

The judge pounded his gavel on the desk, attempting to restore quiet. "Order! Mr. Cates, either sit down or you will be removed!" he threatened loudly.

By now Bryant was on his feet and waving his arms at the judge. "No, Your Honor," he called out. "Please, I'm sure Inspector Cates means no disrespect . . ."

But Cates and Reggie were engaged in their own private dialogue.

Reggie scrutinized Wilson and shook his head. "No, it's some other guy," he told Cates.

"Right over there!" Cates yelled, as if Reggie hadn't already answered his question.

The D.A., secretly pleased that Jack Cates was showing his true colors, pretended indignation. "What's going on? Your Honor," he protested vociferously, "I must object to this breach of conduct and procedure!"

The judge didn't even bother to rule on his objection. Holding his gavel aloft like a weapon, he shouted, "Inspector Cates, you are in contempt of court!"

Jack saw his last hope disappearing down the drain like used-up bath water. "Well?" he urged. "Come on, Reggie!"

"That's not him, Jack!" Reggie said stubbornly.

"What do you mean, it's not him? It's gotta be!" Cates insisted.

"I mean, that's *not* the guy."

"Are you sure?" said Cates, sounding desperate. "That's gotta be the Iceman! People change—"

"Counselor!" roared the enraged judge. "Control your witness or I'll have the bailiff remove him from the room!"

"Your Honor," Bryant entreated, "my client has been under undue pressure due to extenuating circumstances—"

"Your Honor, I must again object. This is utter nonsense!" argued the D.A., raising his voice to be heard above the furor in the courtroom.

"You don't forget guys you robbed half a million dollars from," Reggie muttered under his breath to Cates. *"It ain't him."*

Cates felt as if he were being sucked up by quicksand. "Goddammit! He's gotta be!" he said hoarsely. "He's gotta be the Iceman!"

Abandoning any pretense of being able to regain control, the judge stood up and tried to salvage a measure of dignity. "This is too much!" he declared ringingly. He banged his gavel one last time and glared at Cates. "This court rules that there is sufficient evidence to proceed with a criminal trial against Inspector Jack Cates. Trial date will be set for the earliest opening on the court calendar. This hearing is adjourned."

Long after the judge had left the room, Jack continued to rave about Wilson. Bryant hurried over and tried to calm his client, but it was no use. Jack brushed him aside as if he were a pesky mosquito. Eventually Bryant threw up his hands, shook his head resignedly, and disappeared out the door.

Nor did Jack's colleagues seem to know what to say to him by way of consolation. A few of them patted him on the back on their way out. They knew he had little chance of clearing his name.

Jack finally ran out of steam and shut up in mid-sentence. His shoulders sagging with disappointment, he sighed noisily and stomped out of the courthouse. For once, Reggie kept his mouth shut as they walked to the car. He wasn't sure where they were going, but he knew better than to ask.

Wrapped in morose silence, Jack drove more slowly than usual, chain-smoking all the way to the station house. His face was lined with fatigue as he hauled himself out of the Caddy. Though he didn't invite Reggie to come in with him, Reggie got out of the car and followed him into the building. Only once they were inside did Reggie finally speak up.

Glancing sideways at Cates, he said, "Where are you taking me? We should be out on the street—"

"What's the use?" Jack asked disconsolately. "They got my badge for good. After a criminal trial, I'm a convict like you, Reggie."

Great, thought Reggie. His black ass was still on the line, and Mr. Macho was having a nervous breakdown. "Hey, I'm sorry the guy wasn't in there," he said with a hint of irritation. "But look, it's not over yet. I got connections. We're still in the ball game."

"Forget it. It's over. I'm screwed. Come on . . ."

Jack turned a corner and walked into the squad's locker room, which was badly in need of a paint job and smelled of dirty socks and unwashed jockstraps. He stood in front of his locker and gave a quick twist to the hasp of his combination lock.

He didn't have to bother turning the numbered dial on the face of the lock. It was already open. Jack grinned sheepishly. "I keep forgetting the combination," he explained.

Reggie was pretty sure that Cates had gone mental on him. The thing to do was to stay cool and be tough, he decided. He crisscrossed his arms and said disgustedly, "Come on, Jack. I don't want to watch you clean out your locker. Let's get out there on the street. We still got a shot at this thing."

Jack ignored him. He opened the locker door and began rooting through the layers of possessions he'd collected over the years. He pulled out a bundle of dirty shirts, then a battered black shoe, and finally a large paper grocery bag, folded and taped at the top.

"I went out there once," Jack said into the locker.

Reggie wasn't sure he'd heard him right. "What're you talking about? Went out where?"

"When you were at Quentin," said Jack, turning to face him. "Before they transferred you. I went out to look you up."

Reggie leaned up against the locker and looked bored. "I don't remember seeing your ass."

Jack shoved his hands into the pockets of his pants and stared at the floor. "Didn't go in. Couldn't bring myself to do it," he sheepishly confessed.

"Yeah, right," said Reggie, making it clear there wasn't a chance in hell he was believing this jive.

"I felt screwed," Jack went on, trying to look Reggie in the eye. "I felt I trusted you and you let me down."

"I let you down?" Reggie rolled his eyes heavenward. *Give me strength, Lord.* "That's a good one."

"Hell, I thought what we did, catching Ganz, meant something," Jack admitted. "That it might have even changed something in you—in both of us. Then I get out there to the prison and they tell me you boosted the payroll. How was I supposed to feel?"

"You were supposed to have faith in me," Reggie snapped.

"Yeah." Jack nodded wearily. "Maybe I should have. I was wrong."

He handed Reggie the paper bag.

Reggie held it up at arm's length, wondering whether it contained last month's brown-bag lunch. "What's this?" he said suspiciously.

Jack's eyes were red-rimmed and bloodshot, but he could still summon the energy to crack a smile. He said, "Your four hundred seventy-five thou."

Reggie stared at Cates for a brief moment. Then he gingerly unfolded the top of the bag and peered inside. For once, Cates wasn't shitting him. The bag was crammed full of high-currency greenbacks, held together with rubber bands, just the way Reggie had left them.

Exhaling in a long, sharp whistle, Reggie stared from the money to Cates and back again to the money.

Suddenly Reggie was hit with an appalling insight. "You kept my money in your locker?" he asked Cates.

"Yeah."

"A *police* locker?"

"Yeah, well, you're welcome," Jack said grumpily, dumping an armful of clothes on the floor. "You got no more ties to me. You're a free man, Reggie."

Reggie sighed with contentment and hugged the bag to his chest. Sometimes life could be *so* sweet. The future, with all of its infinite possibilities, beckoned to him like a pretty girl on a summer's night. But his euphoria evaporated abruptly when it dawned on him that there were still a couple of bikers out there, gunning for him and Cates.

"Wait a minute, Jack. Just because I got the money, I'm not giving up on this thing," he protested. "Maybe the bad cop just works for the Iceman. We can still catch him."

Jack was just too damned tired and discouraged. "The trail's cold, Reggie. We're out of gas. It was a good run. But it's over. It's over." He gasped. Cates searched for a cigarette lighter.

"Are you sure?" Reggie asked, picking up the bag and resting it on his lap.

"Yeah," Cates mumbled.

Staring at Jack, Reggie said coolly, "I'm gung ho. I don't give a fuck."

"I know," Jack said.

With that, Reggie stood and walked away, leaving Cates alone.

13

Burroughs lived in a first-floor apartment in the Mission District. When he'd moved in three years earlier, he'd bought himself an expensive deadbolt lock that was supposed to be as close to burglar-proof as any locksmith was willing to guarantee. But he hadn't thought to ask the locksmith how it would hold up under gunfire.

When Hickok and Cherry dropped by, they didn't bother to ring the bell. One powerful round of Hickok's street sweeper was all it took to rip the lock apart.

Burroughs was sprawled out on the couch, watching TV. He had just popped open a can of beer when the deafening burst of gunfire made him leap to his feet. A trickle of beer spilled down the front of his shirt as the two bikers threw open the door and stormed into his living room.

Hickok gave Burroughs a thumbs-up. "How's it going?" he asked, leveling his street sweeper at Burroughs. He looked around the shabbily furnished room. The place was a mess. Burroughs obviously wasn't expecting company.

Burroughs glanced from Hickok to Cherry, who was armed with an automatic that was also aimed in his direction. "I've been better," he admitted.

Cherry told Burroughs what he already knew. "The Iceman whacked out Price."

"You want to talk about it?" asked Hickok.

"Man had no choice," said Burroughs, trying not to show his fear. "Your girl ratted him out to the cops."

Hickok shook his head. "Bullshit."

Burroughs saw the glimmer of doubt in his eyes and felt more confident. "That's right, baby," he said. "You both know her. She dances for a living and lives in the old King Mei Hotel. You two ought to be a little more careful who you hang out with."

The bikers exchanged glances, then looked back at Burroughs. "Who pulled the trigger on Price—you?" Hickok asked.

The answer was yes, but there was no way Burroughs was about to admit it. "What difference does it make who pulled the trigger?" he said coolly, hoping he could reason with them. "The cops were getting close to him. That's the way the Man does business. Business, not personal. You better learn the difference."

"Business?" Hickok pretended momentarily to consider the idea. He was smirking as he pulled the trigger. The bullet whistled across the room and separated Burroughs's ear from his head.

Burroughs fell to his knees, yowling with agony. He slapped his hand to his head to staunch the blood that was flowing freely. A ragged piece of skin flapped above the exposed bone fragments.

"That's business, too," said Cherry.

Burroughs grabbed a pair of underpants that was lying on the floor, pressed it against the side of his head, and staggered to his feet. "You feel better now?" he asked, managing a weak shadow of a smile. "You're still on the job . . . that didn't change the job. You still got to get Hammond."

"How're we gonna do that?" Hickok demanded.

"Kirkland Smith. That was the name of the guy that kept Reggie alive inside when there was papers out on him."

Burroughs's makeshift bandage was soaked through and more blood was beginning to drip onto the floor. He talked quickly, hoping they'd hurry up and leave before he passed out from the pain.

"Reggie owes him, and I figured out where he's going to pay back. His daughter works in a Goodwill store in the Haight, just off Central."

Fingering the teardrop tattoo on his cheek, Cherry leaned toward Burroughs and said, as if he were sharing a secret with him, "You know what we're gonna do? We're gonna get Hammond and the cop and the Iceman and we're gonna kill 'em all and take the money. How's that sound?"

"You stick to Hammond. That's the job."

Hickok's earring bounced merrily as he cocked his head and grinned at Burroughs. "It's gonna be a party, and you're not invited," he said.

Then he opened fire and wasted Burroughs with a

blast of double-ought shot that left the Iceman's messenger plastered against the far wall.

Reggie hadn't wasted any time before telephoning Kirkland to ask where he wanted the money delivered. Kirkland's answer surprised him. He had a daughter who worked at the Goodwill store. He wanted her to have the money. Somehow the picture of that mean old bastard feeling generous with his relatives didn't add up. Reggie shrugged. Live and learn. Sure, he could find the place, he told Kirkland. He'd get right on it.

There were only a few customers in the store when Reggie showed up. He looked around for Kirkland's daughter. Except for an elderly man rearranging the merchandise, the only other employee was a pretty, young black woman behind the cash register. She had beautiful, smooth dark skin, a pouty lower lip that begged to be kissed, and brown, wavy hair that crinkled around her face.

Kirkland's daughter? No, Reggie decided. Impossible.

His eyes widened when he read her name tag: Amy Smith. Would wonders never cease?

The girl finished ringing up the customer in line ahead of Reggie, then turned to him with a sweet, open smile. Reggie hoisted his brown-leather satchel onto the counter and pulled open the clasp.

She glanced inside, expecting to see a jumble of items to be donated to the store, and gasped at the sight of so much money. "What is this?" she said with a wary frown.

"Seventy-five thousand dollars. Your father wants

you to have it," Reggie told her. He guessed her to be in her early twenties, and he liked her voice. It had a warm, friendly lilt to it. Kirkland's daughter! Son-of-a-gun!

"I don't want it," she said, pushing the satchel back at him. "If this money comes from Kirkland Smith, it's got to be dirty. I don't want any stolen money."

Reggie considered what she'd just said. The money *was* stolen, but not by her daddy. The girl's clothes were neat and clean, but obviously on the cheap side. She couldn't be earning very much at a Goodwill store. What the hell? he decided.

"We both know your father isn't a saint, but he didn't do anything illegal to get this money," Reggie assured her. "He kept his word. Kept me alive in prison for five years. Now he wants you to have the benefit of it."

"And this is going to make everything better? Giving me money is going to take care of him not being around?" Amy Smith demanded indignantly.

"He knows it don't. It's just money. But it helps. Look, I never had that family stuff, either, but your old man is trying. A lot of guys never even do that."

Her eyes softened and she turned away briefly. When she looked back at him, Reggie thought he saw a trace of tears.

"I'm sorry," he said gently. "I've known your father for a couple of years and I . . . I know this sounds funny, but you're a very attractive girl."

She smiled. Her smile was like sunshine. "Hard to believe, huh?"

Reggie smiled back. "Considering your father, I was thinking more like *impossible* to believe."

Amy reached for the satchel. "I . . ." Her voice trailed off. Then she remembered her manners and said, "Thank you, Mr.—?"

"Hammond. Reggie Hammond. You're welcome." Reluctantly, he headed for the door, but she called him back. "Mr. Hammond?"

"Yeah?" he said, stopping dead in his tracks.

"How is he?"

"Good. Getting old. You could maybe go see him," Reggie suggested.

She tugged at one of her curls. "Maybe."

"You know, I go up to see him all the time," Reggie lied extravagantly. "Maybe I could take you for a visit."

She smiled again. "Maybe . . ."

Reggie turned to leave. Just then the doors sprang open and he found himself staring down the barrel of Cherry's automatic.

"Three times you been lucky, Reggie," Cherry snarled. "Now your luck's all run out."

There were frightened screams from the customers, and the elderly clerk scurried behind a display of kitchenware. The biker paid no attention to them as he used his gun barrel to shove Reggie toward the back of the store.

"Hey, Cherry, been a while," Reggie said affably, reaching under his jacket for his gun.

"Don't even think about it!" Hickok's voice roared out in back of him.

Reggie turned to see that Hickok was standing behind the counter. He had his revolver aimed at Amy Smith's head.

The boys had outsmarted him. Admitting defeat, Reggie sighed and raised his hands above his head.

"Time to settle things up, Reggie," said Cherry, stepping forward. "Know what I mean?"

He raised his gun and smashed the butt sideways against Reggie's jaw.

Reggie grunted as he slid to the floor. After that, the room went dark.

•

Jack was clearing out his desk. He'd been at it for what seemed like days, but had actually been only a couple of hours. Most of what he was finding in his drawers was junk that went straight into the garbage. There were old files covered with dust; a picture of Elaine, taken before their wedding, when she was still smiling; a mud-caked sneaker that had once been a vital piece of evidence. Why the hell had he held on to all this crap? he wondered.

He'd just started on the last drawer when Kehoe wandered over and plopped down in Cates's chair. "Sorry I couldn't help, Jack," he said.

Kehoe was an asshole, but he was an okay asshole. Jack appreciated the sentiment. "Not much you could have done," he said gruffly.

"It's horse-pucky, man." Kehoe heaved himself to his feet. "Wanna grab some beer?"

Jack always thought it was funny how the guys still hadn't figured out that he'd stopped drinking. He dumped a stack of papers into the already overflowing wastebasket and said, "Naw, maybe later."

He could take just so much sympathy, so he nodded at Kehoe, picked up the wastebasket, and went down the hall to empty it.

As he was leaving, Frank Cruise rushed past him and hurried over to his desk.

"You got a bunch of calls, Frank!" Stevens yelled

across the room, then walked over and dumped them in front of Cruise.

Cruise thumbed through the pile of pink slips. One message worried him enough that he grabbed the phone and quickly dialed the number.

Hickok had been waiting at a street-corner phone booth for the Iceman's call. He grabbed the phone on the first ring and skipped the formalities. "We got Hammond," he said.

"Is he dead yet?" asked Cruise, hunched over his phone in the squad room. He glanced around, making sure that he wasn't overheard.

"There's a change in plans," Hickok informed him. "Killing one of us wasn't in the deal. You want this guy dead—we want five hundred G's. That's the price for you doing one of the Brotherhood."

"Wait a minute! What is this shit? What are you talking about?" Cruise shot back. These guys were supposed to be taking orders from him. He had neither the time nor the patience for independent players.

"Deal with it. Five hundred grand or we let Hammond finger you. There's a ghost town on Route Fifteen about fifteen miles out of Modesto—"

"No way. No ambush specials," Cruise said abruptly, cutting him off. "You want more money, I want another place. Indoors. No bikes. Lots of people . . . Yeah, that's good." He grabbed a piece of paper and scribbled down the address Hickok was giving him. "Okay, I'll be there. One hour."

Stevens looked up when Jack passed by the message center. "Jack, this just came in." He held up a sheet of paper. "Some guy, name of Burroughs, looks just like the guy you were after. They just found him dead, down in the Mission. It was a real messy job. Here's his sheet . . . it's a mile long."

Jack ripped the paper out of Stevens's hand. He hurriedly scanned the information. He slapped his forehead, as he pieced it all together. "Shit!" he exclaimed.

"What?" asked Stevens.

"I circulated this guy's picture in the precinct last night—got nothing."

"So?"

"So," Jack said, moving quickly toward the squad room, "Cruise busted him last July."

He was halfway there when Wilson appeared in front of him like an evil genie. "Cates, I got something to say to you," he began, blocking his path.

Cruise was hurrying down the corridor. Another few seconds and he'd be gone. Jack didn't bother responding to Wilson as he tried to shoulder past him.

"Look," Wilson said, grabbing Cates's bad arm, "let's not pretend there's any love lost between us. I just want you to know it still hurts me when I see a man throw away his career."

"It's okay. I understand," Jack assured him, keeping an eye on Cruise over Wilson's shoulder. "Just so we're both on the same team."

Wilson was still smiling when Jack's fist connected with his jaw. The distinctive sound of bone hitting bone crackled through the squad room. Wilson folded like a cheap suit to the ringing applause of everyone present.

14

The Bird Cage was a multi-story sexual smorgasbord. Located just off Broadway in North Beach, it offered X-rated video rentals, a porno theater, peep shows, loud music, and dancing.

Cruise recognized the place, parked his unmarked navy blue police car, and got out of it, checking to see that the car doors were locked. Looping his leather bag over his shoulder, he strolled inside.

The place was crowded, smoky, and noisy. A burly doorman sat behind a counter to the left of the front door.

"Hey, I'm looking for the Cage Club." Cruise shouted to be heard above the rock music.

The doorman pointed to a registration book. "You a member?" he asked.

Cruise shook his head, no.

"You got to join," the doorman told him. "Fifty bucks. Sign in."

"Fifty bucks? For what?" demanded Cruise.

"It's a private club," the doorman informed him. "Hey, come on. It's where the action is."

Under other circumstances, Cruise would have flashed his police badge and walked right through. But this wasn't exactly police business. So he grudgingly took out his wallet and forked over two twenties and a ten.

"Right," grunted the doorman. "And a two-drink minimum. Sign here."

Cruise scrawled a phony name in the book.

The doorman examined his signature. "Over twenty-one?" he asked. "Just kidding," he hastily added, noting Cruise's angry scowl. "Lighten up. Seventh floor. Take the elevator, straight behind the bar."

Cruise had no trouble finding the elevator that was marked CAGE CLUB—UPSTAIRS. When the elevator door opened, out stumbled a very drunk customer. He was hanging on the arm of a beautiful blond woman, who eyed Cruise suggestively as she walked past.

But Cruise had more important things on his mind. He felt for his gun under his jacket and stepped into the elevator.

"Right this way, honey," said the lady elevator operator and slammed the door shut.

Red strobe lights and screeching rock music set the mood in the seventh-floor main room. Strands of tinselly Mylar paper spiraled from the mirrored ceiling, shimmering through the veil of cigarette smoke that hung in the air. The middle of the room was dominated by a twenty-foot-long runway, which extended out into the middle of the room. A line of G-stringed, glitter-coated dancers gyrated up and down the runway in time to the music.

Six massive pillars, their surfaces covered with a glittering mosaic of tiny mirrors reflecting back the pink and red lights, stood at intervals around the room. Small cocktail tables, most of them already occupied by eager customers trying to look blasé, filled the rest of the space.

Reggie was seated at a table toward the back, watched over by Cherry, who stroked his gun as he waited for the show to begin.

"You don't look real happy, Reggie," Cherry said.

Reggie crossed his arms and leaned back in his chair. "You're messin' up big time here, Cherry," he said, trying to sound less nervous than he was. "You ain't gonna win this. You think the Iceman's gonna walk in here so you can shoot him?"

"You got it." Cherry smiled.

"Your brother always said you didn't get enough oxygen when you were born, but I figured you had more brains than this," Reggie needled him. Experience had taught him that anger made a man careless, so he went on. "You and your buddy are gonna get about fifteen feet outside this building before the Iceman cuts you down. And look at you—you ain't even smart enough to have a plan."

If the truth hurt, Cherry didn't show it. "Sure, Reggie. Anything you say. Right, honey?" He nudged a very frightened-looking Amy Smith, who was seated next to him.

A scantily clad waitress drifted by. "How's your drinks?" she asked. "You guys ready for another round?"

"We're fine," Cherry said, fingering the teardrop on his cheek. "Everything's fine. Tell Angel to come by when she's got a chance, okay?"

Cruise stepped off the elevator and into the main room of the Bird Cage. He was immediately assaulted by the throbbing, high-decibel rock music.

Topless waitresses darted back and forth across the floor, dropping off "minimum purchase required" glasses of beer that sat untouched in front of the leering patrons.

For those spectators who weren't satisfied by the dancing girls on the runway, the management had provided a sideshow. Three glass-barred cages flanked the runway, each occupied by a beautiful topless young woman, smiling bravely as she danced to the music.

Cruise squinted at the dancers as he walked by and correctly figured one of them to be Cherry's girlfriend, Angel.

He almost collided with a waitress carrying a tray of empty glasses.

"Sorry," said the waitress. "Hey, look me up later, okay? You can buy me a drink."

As she disappeared into the crowd, Cruise spotted Hickok at a table next to one of the pillars. He sauntered over and was about to pull up a chair when Hickok demanded, "Let's see the green."

"Where's Hammond?" asked Cruise, wanting to be sure that Hickok had kept his part of the bargain.

Hickok gestured to a table across the room.

Reggie noticed him pointing. His eyes narrowed as he recognized the cop, whom he'd met with Cates at the King Mei.

"Who's the girl?" Cruise wanted to know, suddenly feeling uneasy and wishing that Hammond were already dead.

"Just somebody he was with," said Hickok.

Reggie stared at Cruise, wondering what he was doing here. And where was Cates? It was a hell of a time for him to be among the missing.

"This is bullshit," he told Cherry. "What's that guy doin' here? You said the Iceman was gonna bring you the money. I know what he looks like. It's not him."

"You're just tryin' to save your ass," Cherry said with a knowing sneer.

"I told you," Reggie insisted. "You're being set up."

While Cherry tried to decide who was lying, Hammond or the cop, Cruise was ready to do business. "Okay," he said to Hickok. He opened his shoulder bag. "Five hundred G's, okay? Now let me check the merchandise."

Cruise crossed over to where Reggie was sitting, eyeing him closely. He wanted this to be over with. Turning to Hickok he said, "Take him out behind the building and blow him away. Shoot the girl too. Shoot both of them. Just shoot the little fucker."

But Hickok and Cherry had come up with an alternative plan.

"What the shit?" Cruise hissed, as Hickok pulled out his gun and shoved it into Cruise's belly.

"You don't kill one of us the way you did Malcolm," Hickok spat. "We're gonna take you out real big, Mr. Iceman."

Cruise gulped as he felt the gun poke deeper into his gut.

Hickok nodded at Cherry, who smiled and cocked his gun. Amy Smith heard the click and knew she was going to die. She closed her eyes and clenched her fists . . .

"You got the wrong guy!" a voice boomed out behind Hickok. "Don't they, Cruise?"

He swiveled around. Jack stood behind the pillar next to his table. His .44 was drawn and aimed at Hickok's head.

"Hello, Jack," Cates said nervously.

Reggie and Amy jumped up.

Cherry said, "It's Christmas here. We can take all of them. Hammond, the pig, the Iceman—whole ball of wax."

Hickok looked from Cates to Cruise.

"This guy ain't the Iceman," Reggie said to Cherry. "I told you before you dumb shit."

"That's right," Jack agreed. Somewhere between the station house and the Show-and-Tell, he'd figured out that Cruise had neither the smarts nor the balls to be the brains behind this operation. "All we have to do is wait for the real one to show up."

As if on cue, Ben Kehoe stepped through the beaded curtain of one of the peep-show booths. In his hand was a 9 mm Beretta. He glared at Cates.

"Jack, that's him!" shouted Reggie excitedly. "*That's* the Iceman . . . the mother I robbed . . ."

"I really didn't want to believe it," Jack said.

Kehoe shrugged, wishing it hadn't come down to this. "Sorry to disappoint you, Jack."

Once he'd eliminated Cruise as his chief suspect, Jack realized that it had to be Kehoe running the show. For once, there was no satisfaction in having been right. A wave of white-hot rage swirled through his gut. "I just want the Iceman," he told Hickok. "You can take the money and get out of here."

"Jack! I want the money!" shouted Reggie.

"No way," Hickok said. The Iceman killed Price. They would make him pay.

Nobody moved a muscle. There were too many guns pointed in too many directions. A few feet away, oblivious to the impending showdown among the three cops and two bikers, a roomful of horny men guzzled watered-down beer and gaped at the dancers.

Oblivious to the drama in the room, Angel got down from the runway and was replaced by another dancer. She slipped on her robe and was heading for the back of the room when she caught sight of Hickok and Cruise huddled in one corner. A moment later, she spied Cates and Kehoe half-hidden behind the pillars. Then she glanced at Cherry, saw the gun lying on his lap, and Reggie seated next to him. It took her a couple of seconds to put it all together. When she did, she let out a shriek of terror.

Cherry instantly jumped to his feet, aimed his gun, and fired. The glass pillar next to Angel exploded in a shower of glass.

Hickok followed his lead and whipped out his gun, but Kehoe was faster. He blasted two shots into Hickok's shoulder, knocking him backward over the table.

The crowd, frozen for a beat by the sound of gunfire, suddenly went crazy and broke for the door. Patrons, waitresses, and dancers screamed hysterically as they scurried to find cover.

Kehoe tore open his raincoat and whipped out an

Uzi automatic. He pulled the trigger and opened up with a rackety blast of 9 mm bullets. Jack ducked behind a pillar. A spray of bullets zinged past him.

"Amy!" cried Reggie, as Cherry took aim at her head.

She flung herself to the floor. Cherry's shot went wild and shattered a glass cage. The terrified dancer leaped out and raced for the door.

Loath not to do his part just because he was unarmed, Reggie saw his opportunity and seized it. He vaulted over the table and landed on Cherry's back, crashing him to the ground. Cherry's head thumped hard against the floor. He lay back, momentarily dazed. Reggie grabbed his gun and took aim.

But Hickok, blood coursing from his wounded shoulder, scrambled to his feet and shot first. Reggie tumbled under a table just as Hickok's bullet whizzed by overhead.

A wrestler-sized bouncer stormed through the door, shouting, "Hey! What the—"

Hickok and Cherry both turned on him, guns leveled. With two blasts, they sent him tumbling out into the hall like an oversized beach ball.

The air was thick with smoke and the smell of discharged bullets. A hailstorm of lead boomeranged off the walls and floor as the combatants opened up with an unrelenting fusillade of gunfire.

Cates poked his head out from behind the pillar and fired twice at Hickok. His .44 slugs caught the biker in the legs. Hickok crumpled to the floor, still shooting. He missed Cates but hit the mirrored ball above the stage, which exploded into a thousand glittery pieces of glass.

Now it was Cruise's turn to take on Cates. His bullet ricocheted off the pillar, just missing Cates's head. Jack ducked, and Reggie popped up from behind the table where he'd taken cover. He blasted Cruise in the side, spinning him around like a top.

Jack rolled out from behind the pillar, threw himself into a crouch, and plugged two .44 slugs into Cruise's chest. The impact flung Cruise backward onto the stage, where he landed in a greasy pool of sweat, blood, and sequins.

"Hammonnnnd!" shrieked Cherry, unleashing a barrage of bullets, one of which slammed into Reggie's thigh as he fell to the floor.

Reggie pulled the trigger . . . but he'd used up all his shells. Trying to keep the pressure off his wounded leg, he scrambled under a table and scuttled across the floor. Cherry kept on firing, barely missing Reggie and a couple of customers who'd been making a run for the exit.

Hickok lay in a pool of blood, still clutching his revolver. Bullets flying over his head, Reggie crawled over to the biker and pried the gun out of his fingers. Suddenly, to Reggie's horror, Hickok pulled himself up to a sitting position. His face contorted in a death-mask grin, he grabbed Reggie by the neck and tightened his fingers around his throat.

Reggie pressed the trigger and emptied the cylinder into Hickok's heart.

Rubbing his throat, Reggie took a deep breath to steady himself. Then he opened the loading gate and one by one ejected the empty cartridges. As he fumblingly reloaded the new rounds, he sensed a presence behind him. Looking up, he found himself nose to nose with Cherry.

With a speed that surprised him when he thought about it afterward, he raised Hickok's .454 and fired as fast he could cock and pull the trigger. Cherry took the shot square in the chest. His body toppled backward through a mirrored partition and into the lap of a hysterical, screaming showgirl who'd sought refuge from the gunfire.

Kehoe, meanwhile, had Cates pinned behind a pillar, which he was peppering with 9 mm rounds that were tearing away chunks of the concrete. A movement at his feet made him glance down. A sobbing Amy Smith was crawling across the floor, trying to put distance between herself and the dead body of a customer who'd been killed by one of Kehoe's bullets.

"Let's go, sweetpants!" shouted Kehoe. He grabbed the girl by the hair and pulled her to her feet.

Hugging her to his chest, he dragged her forward into Cates's line of vision. Cates saw her and abruptly held his fire. As the smoke cleared, Reggie peered over the side of a table. Kehoe and Cates had each other at gunpoint.

Cates glared at Kehoe across the battlefield. "You set me up!" he furiously accused the other cop. "You never ran any of that shit through N.C.I.C. You had Cruise pick up the gun at the track that day."

Keeping the girl close to his chest in case Cates got any smart ideas, Kehoe yelled back, "I needed leverage on you, Jack! You were getting close! I didn't think that was necessary . . ."

Jack shook his head. If there was one thing he

couldn't figure, it was a dishonest policeman. One cop gone bad could stink up the whole goddamned department. "Why, Ben?" he asked, truly puzzled.

"Come on, Jack," Kehoe said impatiently, annoyed by Cates's naïveté. "We were fighting a war we couldn't win. I just defected to the winning side. If you're gonna do the job, do it right. All the way. *You* taught me that. I made a lot of money. Now I'm gonna walk out of here—or the girl dies."

Out of the corner of his eye, Jack saw Reggie slowly working his way up behind Kehoe. "Kill her," he said, stalling for time. "I don't give a damn. I don't even know her."

"Good try, Jack," said Kehoe, wondering whether Cates meant what he was saying.

"Iceman!"

Kehoe whirled around. Reggie's gun was aimed at his head.

"It's over!" shouted Reggie.

So he thought. But suddenly a bloodied hand grabbed him by the shoulder and spun him around. There stood Cherry—dripping blood, battered, and seemingly risen from the dead.

Cherry shoved his pistol into Reggie's face and said, "Fuck you, Hammond."

He pulled the trigger. Click. The cylinder was empty.

Reggie smiled. "No," he said. "Fuck *you.*"

Click. Another empty cylinder.

Cherry smiled.

Reggie charged with the full force of his anger, ramming headfirst into the biker. Cherry staggered backward and flailed his arms to regain his balance. But Reggie flew at him with a swift, well-placed jump kick that sent Cherry crashing through the window. He screamed as he plummeted seven stories down to the street below.

By the time the driver of the bottled-water truck saw him, it was already too late to slam on the brakes.

Reggie leaned out the window and stared at what was left of Cherry Ganz. A moment's diversion was all Kehoe needed. He threw Amy to the floor and grabbed Reggie.

"Here's one you give a shit about, Jack," he said, shoving the Uzi up against Reggie's neck.

Jack slowly moved in on them, his gun leveled. "You're a disgrace, Ben," he growled. "Nothing worse than a bad cop. It turns everything upside down."

"Jack, we can work this out," said Kehoe, thinking about Cates's reputation for being a crazy man who would stop at nothing to get his mark.

Jack quickly sorted through his alternatives. His mind made up, he said, "I'm sending you away, Ben. Forever."

"This is just great!" shouted Reggie. "I ain't got no money. Ain't got no car. But I do got a bad-breath motherfuckin' drug dealer with an Uzi stuck in my face, gonna blow my fuckin' brains out! I knew I was gonna end like this when I went out with your sorry ass again. Why don't you just shoot me, Jack? Get it over with!"

"Shut up!" Kehoe screamed.

"Just shoot me before this motherfucker puts a bullet in my brain," Reggie yelled, trying to distract Kehoe. "With my luck, I wouldn't even be dead, and I'll be some fuckin' vegetable, and you could come over to the hospital and unplug my fuckin' machine for fun, you big-ass cop . . ."

Jack pulled the trigger. Reggie's mouth opened in shock and amazement as he felt a searing flash of pain in his gut and realized he'd been shot.

Kehoe saw that he'd underestimated Cates. "You're crazy!" he shouted, raising his gun.

But Jack was faster. He emptied his last five bullets into Kehoe's chest and stomach. Kehoe was dead before he hit the floor.

Jack hurried over to check on Reggie, who lay clutching the right side of his stomach, which was seeping blood. Amy knelt next to him, sobbing uncontrollably.

"You fucking shot me," Reggie said, gritting his teeth against the pain. "I can't believe it."

"Just winged you," Jack said, sounding far less worried than he felt. "They'll patch you up."

"You fucking shot me," Reggie said again, half in anger, half in admiration.

All of a sudden Jack became aware of the girl at Reggie's side. "Who the hell are you?" he asked tersely.

"A friend of Reggie's," she said, biting her lip to keep from crying.

Reggie reached up and grabbed hold of Cates's jacket. "Jack, stay away from my women. You hear me?"

Jack smiled. Reggie was going to be just fine.

Strapped to a gurney and hooked up to a set of I.V. tubes, Reggie was still giving Cates a hard time. "I can't believe you fucking shot me," he said. He winced as the medics lifted his gurney into the ambulance. "Shit! This hurts."

"Aw, you did good, Reggie. Doc says you'll be fine," Jack promised, leaning over him. "Guess I'm a pretty good shot. You're just gonna have to take it easy for a while."

Reggie coughed and pain knifed through him. "I was supposed to be takin' it easy. I knew this is where I'd end up when I went out riding with you, Cates—half dead. Shot my suit all to shit."

Jack, whose face was haggard with worry, matched his tone. "You needed a new suit, anyway."

"How am I gonna buy one? Bikers took my money," Reggie complained, much more upset about the lost money than his abdominal wound.

"Maybe this'll make it up to you." Jack smiled and held up Kehoe's shoulder bag. "I got this off of Kehoe—another five hundred grand for you."

Reggie's face relaxed into an ear-to-ear, shit-eating grin.

Jack smiled back at him. "I'll meet you over at the hospital," he growled, pleased to see that Reggie's spirits had picked up. "We'll discuss it."

He stood up to go, but Reggie grabbed him by the lapels and pulled him back. "Wait a minute," he said. "I'm sorry you had to kill your friend, Jack."

Jack looked at him for a long few seconds. Finally he said gruffly, "That's okay. I had to save my partner."

Reggie was still smiling as the medics closed the doors, turned on the siren, and sped off.

As the ambulance pulled away, Jack pulled out a

pack of cigarettes and reached in his pocket for his lighter. He dug deeper, tried another pocket, then a third.

Jack turned to stare after the ambulance, hurtling through the night toward the hospital. Some things never changed. Reggie Hammond had gotten the last laugh.

Chuckling softly, he slapped his thigh and exclaimed, "The son-of-a-bitch stole my lighter!"